Nothing Rhymes with Orange

The University of Sydney Anthology

Foreword by Katherine Brabon

University of Sydney

First published in 2025 by the University of Sydney.

Funded by the University of Sydney, Faculty of Arts and Social Sciences, School of Art, Communication and English.

Sydney University Press
Fisher Library F03, University of Sydney
NSW 2006 AUSTRALIA

Email: sup.info@sydney.edu.au
sydneyuniversitypress.com

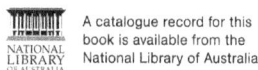

ISBN: 978-1-74210-580-2 (paperback)
ISBN: 978-1-74210-579-6 (epub)

Cover image and design: Shaan Lloyd
Text layout: Hanna Holford and Urvi Agrawal

We acknowledge the traditional owners of the lands on which Sydney University Press is located, the Gadigal people of the Eora Nation. We respect the knowledge embedded forever within the Aboriginal Custodianship of Country.

Contents

Contents

Acknowledgements

For our 2024 anthology, *Nothing Rhymes with Orange,* we gave writers the pen to tell us how they see belonging. From the many responses to our open call for submissions, we selected twenty works of prose and twenty-three works of poetry. Some trace feelings of uncertainty when we are away from what is familiar. Some address the anxiety we feel trying to fit ourselves into a new place. Some cover the connections we share with each other, despite our differences.

Firstly, we extend our heartfelt thanks to our authors for showing us what belonging means to them. Thank you for submitting your wonderful pieces. Without you there would be no point in producing this anthology.

We would like to thank Katherine Brabon for penning the opening to our anthology. Thank you for your generosity in writing our foreword and showing your appreciation for the worlds in this anthology. We couldn't have hoped for a better introduction than yours.

A huge thank you to Dr Agata Mrva-Montoya, our biggest supporter, for giving us the chance to test our editorial skills on this project. Without your passion and selflessness this book would not exist.

Thank you to our editors who all worked tirelessly, jumping in when needed or when somebody was seeking help.

Thank you for spending hours and hours bringing this project to fruition.

We are grateful to the amazing team at Sydney University Press for helping us produce this anthology and to the University of Sydney for funding the project. We hope this tradition will continue for many years to come.

Lastly, we would like to thank our readers, each and every one of you, for supporting emerging writers and editors by picking up this anthology.

Thank you all for your support.

Foreword

Katherine Brabon

I welcomed the opportunity to read this collection and reflect on the compelling themes of alienation and isolation, belonging and connection. These couplings are necessarily interlinked; one a panacea to the other, one longed for while in the other state. In interesting ways, the concepts overlap and coexist.

I became a mother this year. To be alone with a new baby for long hours each day – and in winter, no less – is to experience the strange coexistence of the twin states of isolation and communion. Despite the constant company of a young baby it is nevertheless possible – indeed so common – to feel isolated. The cold, dim mornings seemed nearly indistinguishable from the long and wakeful nights, feeding my son in the quiet of the living room; the stillness disturbed only by his newborn snuffles and the padded claw footsteps of our cat wandering through the room, roused by this new nighttime activity. My partner was back at work after two weeks, so the days also became a strange mixture of stillness and overwhelm, the isolating quiet punctuated by bursts of crying and difficult naps – and, gradually, longer and longer walks to the most pram-friendly cafes I could find.

Around week ten, I went to the first local parents' group meeting organised by the local council. It was a long walk to the venue and I wondered if I had the mental energy for conversation. I won't sugarcoat those first encounters to paint a picture of instant connection. At the first meeting – where the babies ranged from seven to ten weeks old – I think we were all in the bewildering blur of the first weeks of parenthood. My son was quite unsettled for most of the session and cried for the long walk home. I arrived home on edge, and that night told my partner I didn't think I could go back the next week. Somehow, across the next six days, I convinced myself to go. The walk didn't feel quite as long this time. My son slept in the carrier against my body, finally peaceful. The conversations came more easily. A few of us exchanged phone numbers, realising we lived close by.

That first winter – somehow both long and fast – passed. Now we are entering our babies' first summers, and although many of us are still not getting enough sleep, and are frequently overwhelmed by new and old challenges, we're now friends. We're honest with each other, which is what I value most. I can see these fellow parents on a difficult day and they know how it is.

It surprised me that I continued reading so much in the first months of postpartum; I had assumed I wouldn't have the desire or energy. But I found myself reading slowly but voraciously during naps or listening to audiobooks on walks. I see a similarity between the comfort I found from fellow parents and the reading I was doing. This collection, *Nothing Rhymes with Orange*, is a stirring example of the connections and contradictions of isolation, being alone, and the consolations of literature. I am reminded of James Baldwin's wisdom: "You think your pain and your heartbreak are unprecedented in the history of the world, but then you read."

We read about diverse experiences and lives, and we find commonality within differences. As I read the stories and poems in *Nothing Rhymes with Orange*, I was struck by how this collection artfully maps the locations where isolation dwells and finds us: in the home, within families, at the dinner table, at school, in new or familiar environments, in language, in the body. But these are also sites of connection. As the writing moves us through these experiences, the structure of the collection sounds a note of hope, passing as they do from alienation to a sense of belonging and finding one's identity.

Throughout this collection we are shown how words, from a single noun to a fleshed-out family legend, can invite us in, lock us out, shape or dismantle our sense of identity. In "Chrysanthemums" and "Con Ma", for example, we feel the potential of words to both nurture and alienate. There are many other moments of echoing and resonance between the pieces, offering a pleasing beat of recognition – yes, I know this, and they do too. Another example asks us to consider the meaning of belonging itself, and how can we ever reconcile this with our absolute, irreversible separateness as beings in our own bodies and minds. In "The Inferno of the Living" the author reflects that belonging "begins at a bridge between / an outside and an interior, / boldly questioning the liminality / of one and many." Towards the end of the collection, "The Same Blade" movingly reflects on the nature of inheritance and identity: "it's not me to her, not her to me – it is beyond our two / insignificant bodies of water. / we belong to the ocean, she told me once, / and i understood." And of course, in the eponymous poem "Nothing Rhymes with Orange", we are reminded that our essential isolation, the deep interiority of our lives, has beauty in singularity: "Unique, by virtue, is alone. / nothing rhymes with orange."

I invite you to bring your own authentic self to the reading of this collection; bring your honest isolation, your desires, your difficult days – it will reflect yourself back to you wherever you currently are on the pendulum of alienation or belonging. I congratulate all of the authors and editors on this beautiful exemplar of literature's open-heartedness and consolation. To end by quoting one more of the wonderful pieces in this collection ("Where I Made You Happy"): "there is a life, not this one . . . where we lay the doors wide open / let the world's strange magic in." Let the "strange magic" of these worlds beguile and speak to you.

Grave Digger

Natarina Ramdhana

Dear God,
When you die and your body is buried six feet underground, when your flesh has melted into dust and your bones into sand, what becomes of your physical reminders? The objects you left behind that still have your soul imprinted onto them? When the last person in the universe who remembers you passes, these objects wait in the shadows of the mortal world, outlasting your own spirit.

Do you then *cease* to exist? If no person can recall who you were as a person, or your name, did you really exist? One day, marked graves will erode into unmarked ones and the only reminder we will have left in this world is the crumbled pebbles that hide amongst long blades of grass.

Or do you *continue* to exist? Unbeknownst to the living. Do you exist in a sun-bleached polaroid, tucked away and hidden underneath a floorboard? Do you exist in the crumpled soda can, drunk from many years ago, that is now lost and adrift at sea? Do you exist in the flowers once planted in a garden, now wild and overgrown? *Did* you exist?

* * *

These were all questions I had when the bodies started to appear at my door.

The first Tuesday of every month, at exactly 6 am, I would look down the long driveway leading up to my property and squint my eyes against the rising sun. I would see a large truck kicking up orange dust, a benevolent sandstorm.

The truck would pull up next to the barbed wire fence I had set up around the house and its tinted windows would roll down to reveal a single weathered face. The wrinkles that lined his eyes were a bottomless crevice. I feel like they were once the result of a man who had lived his life smiling, but from his dark eyes I could tell that they were now deepened by anguish.

I guess that's how most people look nowadays anyway. He doesn't smile anymore.

The Anguished Man would hand me a clipboard with a government form I had to sign. Our hands would briefly brush over each other as I passed over the signed document, my calluses grazing over his own leathered skin. We never shook hands.

I would begin to unload the bodies.

Sometimes there were five, sometimes there were fifty. Never would I know how many I would encounter when I opened the cargo doors. I would wheel them out into the sun. Dead bodies don't sweat, but occasionally they felt sweaty, and would slip through my arms as I carried them out. At times I thought it was their way of escaping their burial.

When all the bodies had been unloaded, I'd walk up to the truck window and tap on the glass to signal I was done. The Anguished Man would nod. He would start the truck and the rumble of the engine would bounce across the empty plain.

As he pulled away from the house, I'd sit on my porch steps and watch the small dust cloud of his truck grow smaller and smaller, until it faded into the glow of the orange earth. I always wondered what world he returned to. Was it a concrete jungle filled with rubble and the hustle and bustle of thousands of faceless people? I forgot what the city was like.

The sun would be high up in the sky by that point. And with its sweltering rays digging into my spine, I would begin to wheel the bodies into my home.

This is how I started each month after the bombs dropped.

* * *

Dear God,
Who claims the unclaimed besides you? If some people dictate that death only occurs once the living forget the deceased, what does it mean for those who died without the chance of being remembered? Are they stuck in an eternal limbo? For how could you embrace those who passed without being remembered?

I wonder if you only exist because I am alive.

If you only exist because I will it, then I must remember the deceased so they can be guided to you.

* * *

Weeks after the last bomb was dropped, I volunteered to help recover any bodies that were buried underneath the debris. I clambered over mountains of desecrated steel to grasp a bloodied hand sticking out of the wreckage. The hands were always cold.

The number of bodies I found started to pile up. As I dragged my cart of recovered bodies through the city, mounds of inanimate flesh and concrete cornered me. Their mouths

3

were open and frozen in protest, begging for me to join their macabre party. I reeled at the thought of how many lives were gone. Not even just singular lives either but entire groups, communities, families, gone because the powerful held the people at their mercy. Eyes would peek out behind shards of glass, lifeless and empty. The dregs of a life I once knew were dragged behind me on my cart. It felt as if the blood was on all the hands of the survivors.

The remaining government would pay us about $50 for each body that we recovered, as incentive to clean the city and assist the vestigial society with setting up their new life.

So, with my pile of bodies, I took the money and disappeared into the desert. Running away from obliterated memories and the ghosts of a lifelong past. The desert was barren, isolated, and my wasted spirit could haunt its empty country adrift and wailing in silence.

* * *

It was there in the desert that I buried my child, I buried my partner, I buried my friends. And God, I would've buried myself too if it weren't for the Unclaimed.

Because so many people died, there were masses of unclaimed bodies; the dead who no longer had any relation to the living. Faceless and nameless people whose history and lives had been forgotten, whom no one alive remembered or knew. But alas, dead bodies have to be disposed of, and the new government needed to create more jobs.

So I bury them in the desert too.

* * *

Dear God,
Is it okay that I pray over the Unclaimed the same way I pray to you? After I bury them in the scorched earth, I bow my head in prayer. Sweat slides down my back as I clasp my coarse hands. After digging so many graves, my hands are blistered and bloody, so my palms do not touch.

Today when I unpacked one of the boxes of the Unclaimed, I found a string of prayer beads.

* * *

When the delivery of bodies arrived, each body would come with a cardboard box that would have to be unloaded alongside it. Inside would be any assortment of belongings owned (or thought to be owned) by the Unclaimed.

I found a lot of photographs in these boxes. I flipped the soggy pages gently and stared at the different people, frozen in time like insects in amber. There were stories within the pictures and more stories that splintered off into a thousand different directions, buried behind the forgotten faces, waiting to be unearthed. I always kept the photographs I found. If there weren't any, I'd take an item that felt like it had once held importance to them.

I hung their belongings and photographs on my walls. As the years passed and I accumulated more and more to plaster every inch of the surface, I started to paste them on my ceiling as well. Now, as I walk through the hallways of memories, I feel infinite beady eyes staring at me, as if the eyes of Unclaimed are actually inside my house and not buried deep in my backyard. When it gets especially windy and the walls of my house sway a little, the people in the photos seem to breathe.

* * *

I rub my tired hands on the smooth surface of the prayer beads. They are cool to touch, like the small damp pebbles by the river's edge I used to collect with my child on lazy summer afternoons. We liked to stack the pebbles on top of each other, forming cities as miniscule as her hands. And we'd wait and watch as the small stones would crumble back to the bottom of the river as the tide washed our city away.

I admit, I forgot that other people were followers of different faiths. Before I buried the Unclaimed I blessed them the way people of my faith did. I always wondered whether the dropping of the bombs had strengthened people's relationships to God. Entangled in embrace with one another, I imagined them praying like they had never before: "Oh Lord, oh Lord please spare us, save us from this misery." I wonder if their faith deserted them in the final moments when the bombs loomed overhead and they realised that there was no liberation anymore, at least in the mortal world. But maybe from all the hardship they endured, liberation had to come in other forms.

I buried the beads with the Unclaimed body. Today I did not pray over the graves.

I hope you don't mind.

* * *

Dear God,
People have forgotten that our memory is as fluid as the water that rules over us all. The desert does not get much rain but when it does, it floods. Monsoons in the desert are monumental. I watch the storms rage outside my window and from time to time I worry about the graves. The downpour

has washed away the topsoil and the dead clamber out of their tombs. They march to my house and sing shrill songs that grate at my ears while their withered hands constantly knock at my door.

"Do not forget us," they sing.

When the clouds clear and the blazing sun returns, all I can see is empty earth. And I bury the new bodies on top of the old ones.

* * *

They no longer drop the bodies during the day for me to collect; they leave them at the door for me to find.

I found the body of the Anguished Man in the cargo today.

His box only contains a pair of worn leather gloves. When I put them on, they are my size, and I wear them as I dig his grave.

When I return home that night, I walk through the different rooms of my house and gaze at the artefacts of the Unclaimed. I inspect each photograph slowly, making sure to remember the smallest of details of their faces. In bed, I imagine each individual Unclaimed person, playing their images over and over inside my mind like an infinite roll of film.

There is no longer a soul in this universe who knows of my existence.

The body of my Own and the Unclaimed will lie in the gaps of suspended and unsaid words from the sterile and open heart. We will lie with the inanimate stars and the desert that sleeps in between. Our sighs will be heard in the sunsets, but no matter how hard you strain your ears you will not hear our whispers.

The winds will blow sand through the windows and blanket my body and memories of the Unclaimed I have collected.

And the sun and moon will continue to rise and fall.

Amen.

Unfamiliar

Samantha Bowers

Where she is, or who, she doesn't know.
These pink wallpapered halls are unfamiliar.
She doesn't recognise the garden beds, the grand piano,
the creased and withered face inside her mirror.

These pink wallpapered halls are unfamiliar,
like the stranger who drops by and calls her "mum".
The creased and withered face inside her mirror
seems to scream in silent fear, though words so rarely come.

Not like the man, who visits weekly, calls her "mum".
She's never sure how to respond; she tells him "yes dear,"
while inside she screams in silent fear. The words so rarely
    come
and when they do, they judder, jumble out, discordant to the
    ear.

She's never sure how to respond; she tells them "yes dear,"
when they ask her how she's slept, these aproned crones.
Her answers judder, jumble out, discordant to the ear,
her voice so crabbed she cannot place it as her own.

They ask her how she's slept. These aproned crones
don't seem to listen, so she talks about the trees.
Her voice so crabbed she cannot place it as her own;
she thinks the hands she holds are not the ones she sees.

They never seem to listen. When she talks about the trees
visitors adjust themselves in plastic chairs. They change the
    topic.
She thinks the hands she holds are not the ones she sees,
but can't be sure of anything she's grown. Myopic

visitors adjust themselves, in plastic chairs. They change. The
    topic
tiptoed round. She asks it outright, "When can I go home?"
She can't be sure of anything. She's grown myopic.
Her chicks are in another basket, hatched and flown

and tiptoed round. She asks, "Can I go home?"
They say she's there already, but she used to have a yard.
Her chicks are in another basket, hatched and flown.
Who ever dreamt that waking up could be so hard?

They claim she's home already, but she used to have a yard,
she used to have a coffee table. Didn't she? The space to
    breathe.
Who ever dreamt that waking up could be so hard?
The ceiling whispers she can't ever leave.

She used to have a coffee table, didn't she? The space to
    breathe,
replaced with empty space. She water-treads the time with
    chatter,

feeling sealed in, with the whispered inkling that she'll never
    leave.
She tries to play, but learns instead to fight. It hardly seems to
    matter

when you've been replaced. In empty space, she water-treads
    the time with chatter
in the unfamiliar garden beds, or at the grand piano
she tries to play but learns instead to fight. It hardly seems to
    matter
where she is. Or who. She doesn't know.

Consensus

Amalia Stone

Meeting 17542, 1/6/2022, 14:22, attendees: Gabriella, Gabbi, Gab, G., apologies: Bella

1. Gab proposes new gym routine, 5 am, three times a week. Morgana says that's when she goes. Resolved: unanimously in favour, to start immediately.
2. Gabriella proposes leaving, as discussed in previous meetings. Final straw for her: Joe left two voicemails during the big meeting. He knows we hate voicemails, and we don't care what brand washing powder he uses. Resolved: majority in favour, Gab against. To revisit next meeting.
3. G proposes investigating Pyrmont two-bedroom flat. We could walk to work. Kids could stay in same school. To check finances. Resolved: unanimously in favour.

Saturday, 4 June 2022: Gabi's leaving the bed early, second time this week. Joe's too tired to question why.[1] She pulls the sheets back over him, and he smiles with his eyes shut. The

---

1 McGuffin, F. (2021). "Optimum exercise habits in sedentary office workers," *Healthcare Monthly*, 1 April. Gab read this over a coffee break and determined to make a change.

room smells of lavender and he will continue hiding. Kids will be asleep until seven, easy.

He loves these sheets, Egyptian cotton with too many threads, white as on their wedding day ten years ago. He knows the ways of bleach and the sun on the line, but he hasn't bleached them in a while. He stays on his side of the bed, and she on hers. It's just a busy period. Gabi will lose interest in the gym once it's no longer a new shiny thing. She doesn't keep habits forever.[2]

When he makes it downstairs, she's left the coffee machine on and ready to go. Nice. The blend's dark, the way she likes it. He adds two teaspoons of the gritty sugar that she hates.

Meeting 17550, 13/6/2022, 19:45, attendees: Gabbi, Gab, Bella, G., apologies: Gabriella

1. Gab reports new gym routine a success. Morgana sent flowers to the office. Resolved: to continue gym, acquire annual membership.
2. Gabbi supports motion to leave. Last time Joe bought us flowers, they were half dead Mother's Day white chrysanthemums from the corner store. Resolved: majority in favour, Gab against.
3. Bella reports meeting with the bank. If we tap the inheritance from Dad, we can put a deposit down. Worth inspecting the flat. Resolved: unanimously in favour.

Thursday, 16 June 2022: He was sticky from last night, sweat in his chest hair.

---

2   Gabbi would object to Joe's generalisation, but unfortunately, it's true.

They used a condom. He said, but the vasectomy. She said, but the mess. He hadn't wanted to argue, hadn't wanted to get in his own way. Wanted it, even if he finished too quickly, and she took forever, and his jaw still hurt the morning after. Thanks, she said, when she settled back into bed after taking care of herself in the loo.[3] She fell asleep with her back to him. They used to cuddle, he remembered.

In the morning, she left like nothing was different. The gym clothes she wore were brighter than anything else in the room.

He finished his coffee before the kids got up, but with no milk, she didn't pick it up on the way home. A bitter taste left in his mouth.

Meeting 17565, 24/6/2022, 01:45, attendees: Gab, Bella, G., Gabriella, apologies: Gabbi

1. G. presented statement to meeting: although comparisons are odious, Morgana's something to us that Joe isn't even when he's trying. Kissing her is worth the risk. Resolved: unanimously in favour.
2. Motion to leave: Gabriella reports that Joe snored non-stop last night. We got up to look after Simon when he cried at one, he didn't even stir, still mum's job. Joint custody is the default. He'll have to sort it. Resolved: majority in favour, Gab against.
3. Bella will meet a conveyancer on Tuesday. To report next meeting.

---

3   G. used to suffer terribly in her youth: https://aci.health.nsw.gov.au/
networks/eci/clinical/ed-factsheets/urinary-tract-infection-uti-in-women.

Friday, 1 July 2022: The house is almost quiet when the kids are asleep, not completely, possums outside scuttle and the pipes creak. With her out, he feels the night press on his skin. She's been short with him on the phone, *can't talk now, got to go*, her texts are single letter slaps to the face.[4]

He's reading Tolstoy again, stories for the long cold nights, the intricacies of unhappy families.[5] It should be the two of them snugly tucked under a rug with mugs of tea, reading the minutiae of the real, the kids gently snoring in the next room, safe against the imagined wolves. Instead, it's just him and the curated version of their history together. The tapestry hanging on the wall across from the sofa; he doesn't remember what the patterns mean anymore, but he remembers his hand in hers, the flies on his back, South African heat. A carved statue that he insisted they bring home from Hong Kong; probably clever plastic but possibly shameful ivory, the tea that they drank with crackling skinned roast goose, with star anise smoke in the air. Framed pictures of the kids as chubby, smiling babies and toddlers; they should put some more up before they're too wise to know not to smile. A large painting by her mother: a creek tumbling leaves down a waterfall, the leaves hanging in motion like limp wet paper, but Gabi's still a little afraid of her mother, so it stays. The bookcase: her books on the antiques that she would buy if they had more of the ready; his books

---

4   Spratt, V, (2020). "Communication Fail: Please Stop Texting Me." https://www.refinery29.com/en-gb/2020/07/9883862/ text-message-miscommunication. Bella likes to have phones face down at the dinner table, but often work demands more presence. There's a balance to be struck.

5   Tolstoy, L. (1878). *Anna Karenina*. "All happy families are alike, each unhappy family is unhappy in its own way." Gabriella would be hard pressed to say how one determines if a family is happy, but in general agrees.

on mediaeval poetry, Russian literature, and the care of the big dogs that they would have if they lived in a bigger house and the children were older.[6] None of them quite add up to him and her together, to belonging.

She doesn't like it when he waits up for her. She says it makes her feel like a naughty schoolgirl, and not in a good way. He'll try his luck waiting with his book in bed, they really do need to talk. How she feels is up to her to manage.

He falls asleep anyway, to the sound of the rain, where the noise of her snoring should be.

Meeting 17589, 24/7/2022, 05:35, attendees: Bella, G., Gabriella, Gabbi, apologies: Gab

1. Motion to leave: G. notes that Gab would be against, if she were here, but G. supports motion. Resolved: unanimously in favour to leave.
2. Bella reports that the offer on the flat was accepted, closing 26/8/2022. Motion to commend Bella carried unanimously.

Wednesday, 27 July 2022: She rolls over in bed and kisses him, his lips a little prickly, the stubble not yet smoothed out by the blade, and her mouth sour. She pulls back from him, and he takes a moment to appreciate her newly defined shoulders before he wonders what she's looking at. She leans back in to kiss his forehead, leaving the wet impression of her lips behind.

The bedframe creaks as she rolls out and up and off, and he settles back down into the moving mattress. At the door, she

---

6 "What it means when we don't commit to the future." *The Unhappy Marriage Journal*, April 2023. Bella knows, she does.

turns to look at him. He smiles, a little soft one, for the picture she makes: his gym-buffed wife, with the trim waist and the little pert butt, who had kissed him awake. She bites her lip, and then she turns and takes the stairs away.

He can hear the coffee machine as she runs it, smell the dark bitterness of it. Then the dishwasher's door opens and shuts, and that's her putting the cup tidily away. She does like things to be tidy. After a time, the front door closes with a hard knock. One of the children briefly stirs, and then settles. When he makes it downstairs, the coffee machine is off. Cold.

He'll look at the bedframe on the weekend. It might need fixing, they've had it forever and it's too expensive to replace.

Meeting 17589, 1/8/2022, 13:35, attendees: G., Gabriella, Gabbi, Gab, apologies: Bella

1. Motion put forward by Gab to re-open decision to leave. Gab reminds the meeting that he was there during our cancer scare, he was the steady presence when our father died. He loves the kids, cares like no one else, holds the house together even when we're at the office seven days straight. He's funny when we give him a chance, he thinks in a way that we don't, we work together, when it's working. G. responds that dwelling on sunk costs isn't useful when considering future investments, and it's not a reason to hold on to a marriage. Gabbi notes that while we worked together when we were twenty-three, we're different now to the person that promised forever. Gabriella invites the meeting to be honest with ourselves, it's not working now. It hasn't been for a while. Motion defeated.

Gab's objection recorded in the meeting minutes.

Tuesday, 2 August 2022: He timed dinner for the hour before,[7] and made the kids wait. The pasta's solidified into lumps. She said it was none of his business why she was late, not even looking at him, all focus on spooning the yellowy powdered cheese from the white bowl onto the children's plates, little spills on the tabletop.

"How was kinder, Immy?" Gabi said.

Imogen handed her a little card, school crest gold embossed. "It's for reading, I'm the best in my class. Full school assembly."

"Well done," he said. She hadn't said anything at pick up. He'd been up the shops in a café working on a commission, feeling like a grown up, hearing adult voices. "Well done, darling. I didn't know."

"There was a note," Imogen said.

Gabi looked at him, mouth pursed. "I could have gone. I could have rearranged meetings if I'd known."

"I didn't know. I would have gone myself," he said.

"I gave you the note, Dad," Imogen said, poking her pasta with the tip of her fork.

"Eat it," he said. "Eat your dinner."

Imogen looked at her mother with little squints, a little forehead crinkle, and then dissected the pasta into small bits that she could unsuccessfully conceal under her cutlery and napkin.

---

7   Gab knows when Joe's been wafting about all day, because this is what he cooks: https://www.allrecipes.com/recipe/23974/pasta-with-peas-and-sausage/.

"Next time," Gabi said, "give me the note and I'll make sure I'm there. I'm proud of you, Imogen. Well done. Socks up, Joe. I can't be responsible for everything."[8]

"Don't start with that again," Joe said, but she was asking Simon about his day, full of sandpit triumphs and defeats. A little ring of pasta chunks formed under Simon's chin as he spoke. Gabi looked at Joe again as she wiped it up, leaving starchy trails behind, bright yellow cheese powder settling on the gilt crest of the school award.

She was never short with him in front of the children, ever. They were a team. It was understood. Joe retreated to the kitchen with the plates, where she was not. They would talk later, he would explain about the commissions he was taking on, his transition back into the workforce, she'd understand that, at least.

There was a soothing rhythm in the washing up, the scrub of the brush, the scrape of the gluey dissected pasta. A form of meditation, his father once said in the face of a similar perpetually broken dishwasher, rinsing out his mother's endless half-drunk mugs of tea. He placed the last clean plate in the rack, and suds dripped, a line of bubbles formed, rainbows in the kitchen.

"Mummy said she had to go," Imogen said, and the bubbles burst.

"Everything's fine," he said. "Do you have homework? Let's put that award up on the fridge. So proud of you."

---

8   This should be the climactic moment according to the golden ratio, the catalyst leading to catharsis. But marriages don't fall apart like that. Moments roll down hills like pebbles that start a landslide. Gabi couldn't tell you what the first pebble was, couldn't point you to the pivotal pea under the mattress. That's not how she makes decisions.

Later, the kids asleep, he tries to read. Chekov holds no interest,[9] they're not the sort of people who cheat on each other and he doesn't want to read about people who are. He leaves a night light on downstairs, for when she finishes wherever it is that she is that isn't home, and he goes to bed.

In their room, the lavender room freshener is cloying. He unplugs it. The branches in the tree outside keep moving and catching his eyes. He shuts the blinds. A strand from his toothbrush dislodges itself into his mouth. He chokes a little, then he throws up into the basin. Throws up all the mint bubbles, and the pasta, and the bile he's been keeping down, nothing left but sourness.

He wipes the basin clean. Runs the tap and rinses his mouth until the taste is gone, and he goes to bed.

His head lies uncomfortably on the pillow, there are lumps he's never noticed before, patches of dried drool. He turns it over and pummels it into better shape, but a sweet smell persists. Feeling ridiculous, he sniffs at the sheets like the dog they don't yet have, nosing the scent to its source: her pillow. An oiliness to it, something slick and chemical, too sharp to be quite real. He turns that over too, and plumps it up, she'll have to settle into it herself when she returns. It could be a new perfume, or hair gel, nothing he remembers her wearing. He can't remember if she looks any different.

---

9   Chekov, A. (1899) *The Lady with the Little Dog.* "It's not my husband, I've deceived, but my own self! And not only now, I've been deceiving myself for a long time." G. thinks this puts it nicely, even if the lady in the story is a little too histrionic for her tastes.

Meeting 17595, 27/8/2022, 22:35, attendees: Gabriella, Gabbi, Gab, Bella, apologies: G.

Report by Gabbi: the flat is glorious, even full of Mum's old furniture. We've taken the spare sheets; we don't want to sleep on a bare mattress. With all the windows open, you can hear people talking in the pub down the road, and the best of it is that none of them are asking you for anything.

Monday, 29 August 2022: She made him coffee, waiting for him hot and sweet on the counter when he went downstairs. The sweetness carried him through until school pick up. The way in which she woke him in the white sheeted morning, with the pink glow of the dawn blooming through the curtains as he came, her eyes watching, her mouth curved in the smile from their wedding day photos. Her smile kept him floating. It didn't matter that she wasn't home for the supervision of bath time, the blowing of noses and story reading. She said she would be late, and she was late, and later she would be home, and all would be well again.

He pulled their sheets from their bed, the pillowcases from the pillows, the towels from the children's bathroom. If he washed them tonight, he could hang them out tomorrow. Cleanliness, the ruby of wives. Or was that virtue?[10] Fresh sheets always made everyone feel nice, didn't they? Like being in a hotel. Like someone caring for you.

In their room, the children slept, both snoring like little steam trains from either side of their bedroom, little mouths open on their pillows.

---

10 Proverbs 31:10. Gabriella doesn't go to church anymore; she doesn't feel like there's a place for her to belong.

He couldn't find their second set of Egyptian cotton sheets, should be in the cupboard ready to go, he couldn't account for what had become of them. Third best would do, even if they were a bit yellow stained with age, a little ripped at the bottom where his toenails cut through one summer a decade ago, they'd lasted. He would mend them when he got a chance.

Meeting 17595, 1/9/2022, 00:38, attendees: Gabriella, G., Gabbi, Gab, apologies: Bella

1. Motion proposed by Gabriella to reprimand Gab for continuing to sleep with Joe. It's not fair on him. We've made the decision. Your views were considered. Motion to reprimand: carried.
2. Motion proposed by G. to tell the kids, Joe 2/9/2022. Gab asks the meeting to be kind. It's not his fault. Carried.

Friday, 2 September 2022: She said she wanted a Friday night just the two of them. She would pick up the kids, take them to her parents for a night. Meet him at their favourite restaurant, 7 pm. He smiled at the text, gave a thumbs up, and then, after a moment's consideration, a heart emoji, even though she would roll her eyes. So many lovely mornings over the last week, the sheets never quite so well cherished, the way she had held him close, so close that they couldn't see each other anymore.

It would be nice to talk. He wants to talk again, the kind of conversations they once had about postmodernism, and the tensions in the Yugoslav, not just texting each other to pick up milk.

He brushes the stale bitterness of his coffee breath into oblivion, the better to taste the sour fish curry he had always ordered, can taste in anticipation now. It'd been years since they'd been there. Things might have changed.

The Lost Child

Holly May Myers

The seeds of summers were sown,
Sprouting naively from the womb.
Apollo initialled her temple,
With veins in his image:
A vow of vivacity,
Amongst wetlands of lineage.

But her sun-soaked roots desiccated,
As nostalgia lost to the August winds.
Homespun faces contorted,
Disfiguring at her revelation:
"This is a nightmare . . . isn't it?"
Here lies the unspoken conversation.

They held their shears by the blade,
Preaching loyalty at her fell limbs.
But she was dizzy with carbon dioxide
Years before her meristem clung

to the South Coast line.
Where is a tree, if uprooted?

Dew on the Grass

Sharmila Jayasinghe

Trigger Warning: This story contains themes of rape, suicide, abuse and themes related to autism, which may include depictions of sensory sensitivities, social challenges, and experiences of misunderstanding or stigma. Reader discretion is advised. Please take care of yourself while reading.

Dew on the grass.

If someone asked what I missed most about Pembrooke Street, that's what I would say.

Dew on the grass; they had no pattern of life. It sprung in winter, in spring and in summer, but that too at their own discretion. It was at Pembrooke, the cemetery bordering our house, that I noticed dew for the very first time. Water droplets glistened in the sun, holding on tight to the swaying blades of green grass next to the headstone of Mary Martha Lewis, born 2 January 1930, and promoted to glory on 3 September the following year. Sitting on the cement block that kept little Mary Martha caged underground, I watched the glistening bulb of water let go of its grip and slide down to kiss the earth. I wondered if the one-year-old girl would feel the dew drop seeping in through to her permanent abode.

Ours was a big block of land, the last on the cul-de-sac, the one bordering the cemetery. The dead were our closest neighbours. They didn't scare me much; they didn't scare me at all. Maybe it was because my life had truly begun there. There on the cold cement slab that kept Mary Martha Lewis underground.

Kids are like jam jars. Everyone got slapped with a label one time or the other. Labelling started at school, the senses prompted one to label the other. In my class there was a "fatty", a "smelly", a "brownie", a "skull face", a "naughty boy" and a "penis puller", but the trophy for the bearer of the worst label hands down was given to me. They labelled me "rape child" from the very moment I was born. My mother never got labelled a "raped child". Her label was her own name, Luna, just with a "poor" added to the front.

Poor Luna K. Reimers, my mother, was born on 20 July 1969. The excitement of the moon landing had triggered her to slide out between her mother's creamy white thighs into the world forty-five minutes after Neil Armstrong set his foot on the surface of the moon. Her mother had held her close to her heart, given her the first taste of milk, and died of "complications at childbirth", on the same couch she had watched the moon landing on. Grandpa Reimers had been furious with the little brat who caused his wife's death and never learnt to see beyond. He guarded his love, not granting it to a motherless child.

One could have immediately guessed that Luna wasn't born right. I can imagine her being a peculiar kid, kicking and screaming for no reason, flapping her arms like she was doing the chicken dance, and swaying endlessly from front to back as she often did even in adulthood.

"She is not right, Sam. Maybe an exorcism?"

I heard it was Aunty Mable, the one who drove around visiting all her kin to hand over homemade Christmas

Breudher, who was concerned the most. She had kept voicing her opinions until throat cancer robbed her of her voice.

"Nah," Grandpa Reimers had dismissed the notion, always with a wave of his hand. "Just stubbornness. That's all it is."

Luna sometimes shared horrors from her childhood with me, of how her father had beaten her to a pulp with a belt because she forgot to look him in the eye when she spoke. She said she retreated into a shell, likening herself to a tortoise with a star on her shell. Luna was a survivor, that much I know. She survived on her own.

Women who pranced in and out of her father's life had adopted her, but that had been only for that small period of time when they orbited Grandpa's space. She told me some of them were kind to her, and some were not. I deduced that the scars all over her body shaped like shooting stars were a result of the women who weren't kind. I imagined each scar held a story Luna forgot to share. I remember, sometimes Luna would hum a haunting tune and rock herself to and fro, to and fro, when we were alone, a gentle finger caressed her line of scars, like she was willing them to disappear.

Luna was not a Barbie beauty, but with an angular face and thin long limbs, she was pleasant to the eyes. Her hair naturally spiralled as if it had been given attention and shone a brownish gold under the light. Her mother, a migrant of mixed race, had gifted her with that extraordinary colour of skin. Luna was a peculiar type; socially backward and weirdly private, she preferred to be with herself than with anyone else. She didn't have much of anything but the little bit she had she kept neat and tidy. The few pairs of shoes sat in a straight row not touching each other; same interval between each pair. The handful of clothes hung colour-coded inside a thin long almairah. Books were what she owned the most. There were mountains of books of different heights neatly placed next to the bed we shared. She dusted them to a routine and made certain not a speck of dust or dirt remained on them. She spoke of the lives of the book characters like they were her own but rarely spoke of her own life. Though we often walked past the small public school she attended as a child on Gilbert Road, she always looked the other way. It was as if she was angry with the school. When I was tipped to attend the same school, she had become aggressive and had protested like I was given the death sentence.

Luna spoke only when she wished to. Some days she didn't talk at all. There were good days. She mopped, cleaned, cooked and danced the waltz with me, and then there were those days she just sat at the window for hours like she was waiting to be rescued. She screamed in her sleep and kept me awake at night, but acted as if she didn't know. I don't know what I was to her, but I know in her own weird way she wanted to be there for me.

Luna liked routine. She would have always been someone who never veered away from routine. I can imagine her as a kid waking herself up very early in the morning, staring out the window, walking backward five spaces, then standing at the mirror, sliding the brush through her hair twenty-five times, dressing in her pink and white gingham uniform, scarfing down a sandwich with too much vegemite, and crossing the road to walk to her school. She said other kids who walked the same path threw pebbles at her like she was a dog. According to her memory, her morning routine changed a bit only when the headmistress had called her father to school and complained that she wasn't right in her head. "She is scaring the younger kids. I can recommend a psychologist," Mrs. Hanna had offered, but her father had been stubborn.

"Nah, just stubbornness, that's all, no one in my family is cuckoo," he had said, annoyed.

"He beat me black and blue," Luna recalled. Luna had never gone to school again, but her morning routine had still persisted. With no school to attend to, she had idled around the house, humming, reading, and staring out the window.

Luna said it was the fire in the cemetery that had made her happy. She recalled how one day in the cold of winter the bush next to her house had caught fire. She had woken up dead of the night, drenched in sweat and unable to breathe.

"I could see the sky changing colours from my bed, flames dancing, orange, blue and yellow against the sky," she said. Mesmerised by the sight, she had walked to the window and watched men battling the flames. She had watched for hours, and finally, only when the sun shone on her face, she said she had seen a true miracle: "The eucalyptus trees that hid the cemetery before were all gone. Burnt to a crisp and fallen flat, and there they were, rows and rows of dead remembrance stones, standing guard, triumphant like heroes of war."

Luna said that morning she had walked out of her house and headed to the cemetery in nothing but her linen night dress. "I was so happy." She beamed and from there onwards she said, she had added an early morning visit to the cemetery to her daily routine.

"You were conceived in the cemetery," she confessed to me once. "Just one time I did it with him, and boom you grew in my belly."

She had looked back at her life with dreamy eyes before the excitement faded and her eyes became vacant again. It had been on my fifth birthday and we had just finished half of a lopsided cake Luna had baked for me. I was too young to make sense of what the "it" she had done and who the "him" was. Now I regret not asking. "Luna was just a child," I do remember Uncle Neil's last wife declaring one time over dinner. She had said it like it was her story to tell, "She was raped in the cemetery. No one dares visit the cemetery after dark now." I remember Luna's grin, a mischievous one, but when Grandpa Reimers's face went dark, I remember Luna biting her lip and rubbing off the grin.

Luna's visits to the cemetery never stopped, not even when I was born. She held my hand, crossed the road, and walked into the cemetery without fail every day. Inside the grounds, we paced from left to right. Always from left to right, reading the words carved on the stones aloud, beginning with Mable Gray, 1932–1985, "our inspiration, never far from our thoughts" reading in between and ending at Walter J. Walpole, 1913–1973 "Eternally loved and the beloved husband of Nina".

I thought I was close to my mother. With an age gap small enough to be as between siblings, we couldn't have been just a mother and a son. I can't remember ever calling her mum; it was always Luna and Jimmy James.

James was my given name and my surname at the same time, just because Grandpa Reimers refused to claim me as his blood. He wasn't the most pleasant person to be with, he was actually a mean man. He had a foul mouth and a soul more bitter than a gourd. He was a brown man with a white name. His mixed blood had given him fair skin, light hair and cat's eyes. He said his people came from Europe and denied he was an East-West mash-up. "We were the conquerors. We ruled over them for years," he said, wishing to be superior to the natives of Ceylon, the land in the East the West had colonised.

The Reimers had done quite alright in Ceylon under British rule, planting teas and owning estates, but when nationalism rose its head and the government decreed the majority's language as the official language, Grandpa Reimers who was an English speaker had joined the hoards who left for foreign shores in protest. He had been too young and hot headed to understand why he shouldn't leave. He had sold his tea estate for almost nothing and had boarded a ship that docked in Sydney. For years he and his wife had toiled to build the same kind of success he had as a tea estate owner in the hills of Ceylon, but had no such success. When his wife died during childbirth, Grandpa had given up on his dreams and taken to the bottle. Never admitting it was his own doing, Grandpa Reimers had piled up a mountain of hatred towards the brown man who wronged him by sending him away from his home. He hated that I was born brown. My skin colour alone highlighting a secret he wanted to hide.

"You couldn't even get the colour right." Grandpa Reimers put the blame on me like I had a choice in the matter.

"You will never amount to anything," was his anthem. Singing it a million times, with hate-filled eyes burning through my skin. His hatred was equally distributed to me and Luna his own flesh and blood.

"I think Grandpa killed your father and hid him inside the boot of the Morris Minor," Luna had once whispered in my ear. That was the day the father and the daughter yelled at each other showing how much each hated the other.

The neighbourhood I grew up in also had stories to tell to rival Luna's. We were a modest family in a community where everyone knew each other. Everyone's business was everyone else's and when Luna's alleged cemetery rape took place, the community had apparently rallied behind her in goodwill.

They say the media too was involved, with men and women with microphones and cameras flooding the cemetery, gathering bits and pieces of information and weaving a story that was able to entertain a whole nation. According to community legend, I had become a minor celebrity for no good reason. Just as the day I was conceived made headlines, the day I was born too had made headlines. An entire community had been waiting in anticipation for the rape child to be born. According to some, it had been like Christmas in October; everyone eagerly waiting to tear off the wrapping and find out what lay inside. They say when the first wave of pain hit, and Luna had cried out like a wounded animal, Grandpa Reimers had rung for an ambulance and ran to the neighbour's house shirtless and shouting blue murder. Mason Peters, the neighbour, had calmed him down while his wife sprinted up the stairs to be with the child in labour. Luna said she had wanted to give up and *die,* but the urge to poop had been greater than her will to die. So instead of dying, she said she pushed like she was constipated and had borne down a five-pound baby boy at 2.30 pm on 6 October into the gloved hands of paramedic Anjan. How ironic it is that a brown man had to be the first to hold the child no one expected to be so brown.

Grandpa Reimers had taken my birth as an intrusion. He took every opportunity to show me how unwelcome I was. Though soft spoken and well mannered to the outside world, Grandpa Reimers was a different man inside the house. "Hitler reincarnate," Luna called him.

"You shouldn't sit so close to a dying man. His soul will enter yours," Luna said.

The day Grandpa Reimers exhaled like a rusty old engine and failed to inhale back, she dragged me out of his room. She was terrified and ecstatic at the same time. It had happened all of a sudden. One day Grandpa Reimers was full of life, the next day his lung collapsed and his face went blank. Luna didn't panic, she waited till she was certain that his heart had stopped before dialling triple zero.

Soon after, a slab of cement caged Grandpa Reimers underground in Pembrooke cemetery, Luna ran to his room and found the keys to the shed and the Morris Minor car. Kicking off her shoes she hurried down the muddy path, fought with the rusty padlock, and pulled open the rickety wooden doors. I followed her down the path, but with a wave of her hand, Luna halted my advance. Once she was inside the shed, I heard the rustle of keys and the creak of doors and then there was a throaty scream. I was fixed to the ground when Luna returned, pulled me by the hand, and hurried back home. For the rest of the evening, and for two days more, Luna had been silent, pacing up and down the verandah, looking at the shed. I ate what people had stacked in the fridge and made Luna take small bites. She was different, like she was in another world.

On the third night after Grandpa's sudden demise, the stench of excrement mixed with burning wood woke me up in the dead of night. That was the night I was labelled anew; *rape child* became *orphaned child*.

The moon shining through the shutters shone the light on the face of the woman who bore me. Her eyes jutted out like they were escaping their sockets. Her tongue hung from the side of her mouth like a large piece of seaweed, slimy and rubbery. Her lifeless body dangled up above, a white bedsheet and noose around her neck. I was seven years old when I untucked myself from my bed and walked past the dangling feet and stepped out of the house, still in my bed clothes.

Leaving behind my mother dangling on the ceiling beam and a shed burning in the backyard, I climbed over the wooden picket fence and entered Pembrooke cemetery, like it was the right thing to do. When the inferno lit up the skies and the sirens wailed, I laid my head on the cold cement slab that held Mable Gray underground and watched dew blossom.

It was the firies who found me the next morning, lying blissfully amid baubles of dew hanging from green all around me like fairy lights switched on, to celebrate the transition, my new beginning.

So, when people ask me now what I miss most about Pembrooke Street, "Dew on the grass," I say, just because I do not know if I should remember anything else.

Somewhere, Not Here

Soralinn

"Somewhere, not here."

It was my religion, all my life I poured unwavering faith into.
I raised the little girl to find a place that wasn't there –
As long as it wasn't here, dear do you know?
Life would've decorated her with all the right choices.
I navigated the world in five different lingua,
I navigated aimlessly as I swam an ocean to reach another's
    shore.

"Somewhere, not here," I could not find.
Ocean was only one, a connected whole.
Sky was just one, maybe many selfish colours,
I cried, I wailed, with hunched back in the sleepless nights.
"Father, I've come too far. Yet, no place to return."
I stayed on the lowest grounds to bury it in the sand.
Because it is not here that I am meant to live – all the right
    emotions bailed on me.

Like a defeated hero, one whose journey was given up through
    the slippery slopes,
I whispered to my mother in the finest pretense I could.

"It'd be okay here, if I had you."
My father let me know, despite his way of love to not.

"Somewhere, not here, is just somebody, not there."

Closer to Middle-Aged than Zero

Jannet Xie

Trigger warning: explicit mention of suicide, self-harm, mental illness and other distressing themes.

Dear Mum,

I wrote my first eulogy at twelve. I am not sure I even knew what I was doing, but I remember the labelled envelopes and pink satin bows. I used my best penmanship, trying not to disappoint the recipient, even in death. I wrote my first will at fourteen. I had nothing to my name; it was not even legal. But I was thinking about how someone needed to look after my favourite teddy bear.

In Year 10, my best friend forced me to see the high school counsellor. When I told him I was self harming, he told me, "Hey, it could be worse. Another girl I'm helping told me she swallows her blades and it absolutely ruins her." I just laughed and thought about the rusty pencil sharpener blades on the side of my desk, next to the amassed pile of tiny screws and unused plastic. It took me five years before I even thought about opening up to a healthcare professional about anything again.

In the first year of my undergraduate degree, I journalled the sentence, "A shattered mirror would confuse itself, trying to hold my reflection in its arms." To this day, I wonder if I know who I really am, or if I am just a hot-glued disaster of intrusive thoughts and manipulative lies imposed on me by a diagnostic label.

For as long as I can remember, my existence has thrived off others. I was the quiet one in school, letting others take the stage. I had always possessed the intrinsic desire to be accepted by others, to do anything to avoid rejection. If I mimicked their behaviour, their personality, their style, how could I be disliked? Glances from loved ones, glares from strangers; a quick assumption would swallow me. I tried everything, from deteriorating eating disorder behaviours triggered by my mind's need to be the worst of my friends, to pulling all-nighters for a single shred of positive feedback in my assignments. I sought out niche communities just to feel any form of warmth, any escape.

Although the desire to belong is a human trait, the intense depth of my feelings and extreme distress, which often followed rejection, would entirely consume me for days. I thought it was normal, that it was part of the universal human experience. A simple argument would trigger torrential storms. I would sit on the floor with a wine bottle for hours, as though my own heart had stopped. I felt as though grief itself had taken over my body; the loss and abandonment of any interaction was innately personal. People around me would question me, question my reality.

"I don't get why you're making this such a big deal."

"I can't understand you."

"What is wrong with you?"

"Why is this happening again?"

"I'm better off without you, seriously."

"My friend/family/therapist was right about you."

"Why are you being so crazy?"

"So attention seeking?"

"So dramatic?"

"So manipulative?"

"So confusing?"

"So irrational?"

"So controlling?"

Words upon words, sentences upon sentences, arguments upon arguments, until the voice inside my head automated them for me.

After all, I *had* to be evil. I *had* to be bad. I did not deserve anything, anyone. I was not worth it. I would never be worth it. Besides, who am I to deserve anything when I do not know who I am? I am a *fraud*, a fake. I am *nothing*. Everything I have ever achieved will never be enough, will never amount to anything. I will die alone, and it is what I deserve. My best will never be enough, not even close.

Thinking back, how could I have known differently? Growing up as the eldest sister in a second-generation migrant family where mental illnesses were stigmatised and ignored for the sake of saving face, how could I have known the answer? How is that fair? I was just a child. I am just a human. I am just me.

I was diagnosed with borderline personality disorder the day I turned twenty-four. It joined a long list of previous diagnoses, including attention-deficit disorder, anxiety and depression. It made sense, came more as a numbing acceptance than anything else. Still, I cried. Right in front of the psychiatrist I had just met half an hour ago and was paying $500 to see. She just stared at me with disingenuous eyes, not even bothering to pass me a tissue.

Still, I was finally seen.

The decades of failed suicide attempts now made sense. The personality trait of a *cry-baby* was not just because I was the spoilt daughter or a pisces. My desperate attempts to seek attention by running scars up and down my arms when anger overtook me. The volatile friendships and relationships. The black-and-white thinking. The intense self-hatred. The hollowness of my soul. The splitting. The aching need to end it all – to choose nothing over any ounce of desertion.

I write this self-reflection at twenty-five. I know I do not know much. I know my favourite colour is still pink. I know I still love that teddy bear. I know I am still best friends with the same best friend from Year 10. I know I never planned on making it this far, but I know I made it to an age closer to middle-aged than birth. I know I might not know much, but I know that it is okay not to know it all; that it is okay to make mistakes and to feel like the world is collapsing. Because the sun will always rise, whether I want it to or not. The world will continue, whether I wish otherwise. So, I know that I must choose myself, even if I am still just as terrified as I was. Even if I am now double the age I was when I first attempted. This time as I finish writing, however, I will address the recipient as my own name. I know I might not know much, but I know I must choose myself because I know who I would like to be; who I am going to be.

Take care and be safe,

Jannet

P.S. I love you. I always will.

settler gratitude

Hellai Gul

think of those that made you happen
to sit at this table
to ponder luxuriously
homes were forsaken, selves reshaped
gloom faced and mislaid
they forged your dreams to forget theirs

now you must carry gratefulness
for them
and for those that welcomed us on to stolen land

Odile's Feastings

Saraa Purba

I often think about Hilma's swans. It's insidious really: they meet, mirror one another and consume each other in this great spiritual unifier. Where opposing forces live in harmony, where light can only be worshipped once darkness is inevitable. But consumption is never this clean. To be consumed is to lose oneself. To be the consumer is to be parasitic. It's a wretched business and I think I've started to resent the swans.

One with tattered ebony feathers and a yellow beak, the other virginal white with a cherry beak soft as cartilage. They come from contrasting worlds; the young swan begins at the entry point of existence, she emerges from the black sky, her white feathers make the quiet dark seem so acutely loud. Opposite her flies the ebony swan. Much like when one makes it up three flights of stairs, there is exhaustion in her dance across the ivory sky. The naïve young white body mirrors the ebony. The great cycle of love begins once again; as Adam hopes to brush with God and is fooled into submission, consumption is inevitable.

* * *

I remember thc unsteadiness of the cold water in early June as a child, how it left my skin with a nation of bumps like a duck's flesh. The prickly ocean was, however, the least of my concerns as a child. Mother bobbed in the water, her legs not much longer than mine, which was funny to me at the time. She was thirty and I was six. I thought she had left a bag of bones somewhere and hadn't finished growing. But mother was always telling me such bags did not exist. I did not believe her. I remember gripping onto her shoulder firmly in the ocean – what insane person lets go when they don't know what is beneath them? She was determined to "teach" me how to swim, or at least to yell about the concept.

"FLOAT, FLOAT. TRY. Let go."

"I can't. I don't know how."

She begrudgingly let me cling on to her, looking at me with such disappointment, as if the whole swimming situation was a failure on my part.

* * *

The swans are curious about their own polarity, sizing each other up before the great wrestling match. Balanced as it all seems, the white swan reminds me of *Rocky Balboa* against *Apollo Creed*. It's odd really, if you had watched the training montage in isolation Rocky appears in control, with agency; he pulverises frozen meat and consumes raw eggs without gagging. But that is all it is, an appearance. The world is an Italian neo-realist master, and, well, Rocky is just a muse. I've always believed the ebony swan could sense the eagerness in the younger white swan and resented her for it. How dare the withered watch the juvenile prosper? Even if the white swan had danced quietly, the very act of movement is the gallivanting of youth. I wonder though, what there is to despise about the blissful? Does Apollo crave Rocky's unknowing?

Does he wonder what it is to be hungry rather than expected to be great? What privilege is there in postponing the inevitable? The young will decay and the old will die; those states exist in all of us. And so jealousy dilates the black swan's eyes, and the white swan transforms from a familiar stranger to prey.

* * *

Eventually I used all the bones in my bag and grew until I overshadowed my mother. My sister Estha had found about half of hers. Perhaps she had scattered them like an Easter bunny's eggs. Estha never did win those hunts. We used to communicate as if we were forbidden to, as if mother was envious of bliss personified. Snickering relentlessly, I'd beg her to stop speaking, for fear I would have to purchase a lifetime supply of inhalers. The centre light was never on. The warmth of the stove kept our skin glistening. And the glow of the fridge bounced onto the counter so I could see her in the tender darkness.

"And there'll be glass tiles, and majestic trees . . . " I thought of what else to add to the absurdly long list. "And a huge pool!"

"So, you'll sell your soul for this, or is that my role?" My sister burst into laughter.

I liked it then, when the kitchen was quiet, when we were the loudest the world had ever seen.

When we slipped into such noise, Mother always told us to stop fighting. To her, our laughter sounded like war, or a catfight between sisters. So the stove was turned off and we got ready for one of our silent hour-long drives. "Ready" was defined by my best white pyjamas with red stitching. For the world would not see me, but I would be watching *it* intently.

Usually when we went on these drives across the city, its love affair with the weekend had brought it to life. But like all those in unlabelled relationships, the city was in a perpetual cycle of vibrancy and exhaustion. That Wednesday night we avoided its romantic melodrama. It is strange to visit the city when it is comatose. Wednesday often does feel like an itching purgatory. Those keeping the previous weekend alive have given up, and those who start the weekend early are still in a state of beauty sleep. In that sense, Wednesday will never be alive for anyone.

We were always quiet on these drives, we all listened to different music. My sister obsessively switched between songs to capture the "perfect vibe". My parents listened to whatever playlist my father had made five years before (and had been meaning to update for the last year). I would give him the benefit of the doubt; the process of converting a YouTube video to an MP3 file and then putting it onto a USB was an incredibly tedious task.

I always listened to Sam Cooke in the city; his voice was grand, and I was in my Wednesday best. My mother would often watch us from the rear-view mirror, how the flashes of the highway lights rebirthed our faces at rapid intervals. It felt as though she lurked in the shadows of the car roof, but her eyes would always catch strays of the ecstatic lights. I mostly avoided meeting her gaze in this disjointed fashion, for it was better to be sickened by vanishing roads than to be seen. But the hidden are often found if the seeker is lonely enough.

"When I was your age, I had far more hair than you."

"I guess we're different then."

"Some say we look like sisters, but you never let me see you, so how would I know you're not hideous?"

"Does it matter?"

"Matter? I'm your mother. If I don't help you, who will?" My sister had ignored the exchange, my father the same. I sat quietly burning in the car; it was smarter to be meek. Now I sometimes wonder if my mother intended to raise me into a quiet lake. If she resented that when I moved in water, it made ripples.

* * *

There is something curious about ballerinas' backs. How they contort each muscle to pulse with a strength dressed gently. I imagine they swim across the Pacific Ocean in hopes of turning their shoulder blades into wings. How honoured must a swan feel to be envied by a human? Or is any of it particularly important to a creature, made a god, that won't speak to us?

I've got this theory that sometimes Hilma's swans go off book. That once the curtains closed (or rather, the twenty years Hilma forbade the work to be seen after her death) things got aggressive. In 1966 the U.S. Supreme Court claimed, "though the husband and wife are one, the one is the husband". But the seduction of power is not really isolated to our enslavement within the patriarchy. Many fights with white-knuckled fists, or rather stiff beaks, to not be the one that loses themselves. And so, once Hilma steps away, the two swans crawl out of the oil paint sludge and truly have it out. Feathers are tugged and a million quills are made. The black swan's eyes try to escape her in fear of her mind. The white swan becomes grossly aware of her adopted violence as she draws blood from stripping ebony feathers.

* * *

46

In my twenties I found great relief in standing in my kitchen hammering away at chicken. I made a lot of schnitzels at twenty-two. Iris would occasionally watch me from our couch with this expression of queasiness. Her eyes would tuck themselves into her brow bone, and her cheeks would dimple like unevenly baked bread rolls.

"So . . . did she call you?" Iris knew the answer.

"I called *her.*"

"That was nice of you." Her face shrank like a raisin.

I took the bloated chicken out of the sink and began cutting the poor bird open from its nose to backbone.

"Why do I always do this? This guilt, I . . . she doesn't deserve a thing."

"Okay, well, you called, you wished her well. And now we've got dinner with my mum, and she adores you."

"She couldn't even say a fucking thank you."

I remember throwing the scissors into the murky sink water. I had cut myself but persisted with that delicious crack that occurs when you flatten the chicken's breastbone with your bare hands.

"Darling you need a band aid, slow down."

"I'm fine."

She got up from the couch and walked towards me like a zookeeper about to sedate a beast.

"Hey, hey. Look up, it's our kitchen."

Iris weaved her arms under mine, we swayed quietly. Two trees in the wind that found themselves sharing roots.

I wonder now what my wounds took from her. She would bandage them every day, only to find me gnawing at white gauze, soaked wine red. I bled openly and messied our kitchen. Those that show up to Mother's Day without the embarrassment of a charade are the good willing. But what is there to say to someone who is betrayed by their first protector?

Eventually Iris went to the shower. Eventually I finished spatchcocking the chicken. Eventually Iris got tired.

* * *

Youth has a certain air of strength, but jealousy, jealousy is an entirely different drug. The ebony swan makes her way across the bloodied floor, for the first time the pale swan truly fears death. Cornered in Hilma's studio, the white swan falls to her back and the black swan goes for the jugular. She pulls at the young skin with the force of a child tearing through its mother's body. The black swan rips the head of her prey off. A moment of clarity punctures through the violence, she looks at the severed head. They look awfully similar.

* * *

My wardrobe seemed to have nothing in it. Clothing seemed partly meaningless. The sheer defeat of seeing my mother after the incident felt like a betrayal. I covered the *whatever* dress in a distracting white coat that appeared to be shedding and made it to the theatre. There she was. She looked perfectly fine.

"Well, are you going to say hello or is telepathy an option?" Mother found confrontation to be comforting.

"How are you?"

"Good, great if you'd call, your sister would call."

We walked up the steps and the world became awfully slow. She swayed back and forth, and it felt as if I was leashed by a chain to her hand.

As Tchaikovsky's music reached our lips, Mother took it upon herself to perform. Thirty-two fouettés, Odile spins thirty-two times. Estha and I had promised to watch it together on my thirtieth birthday; here I was. She, the black swan, desperately tried to dance as the winner.

"Your sister calls me all the time."

"Called you."

"It's your turn to take care of me."

Tchaikovsky's music grew louder. Odile spun faster.

"My turn?"

"Your sister—"

"Don't you dare use her, you manipulating bi—"

"She loved me!"

The music louder, the spins faster.

"And then she grew up."

"Then what?"

"Then she couldn't take it anymore."

Louder. Faster. The crumpled velvet closed in on us.

"Guilt, you've mistaken guilt for love . . . how tragic."

There I was, bloodied by my own fury. The audience broke into applause, the beautiful ballerina gave them a second chance to love her and turned once again.

I left the balcony disgusted. That every time we spoke, she consumed me. I won't be Odette. I won't sink because she fears ripples in the water.

land & sound

Hellai Gul

no language sounds right in my mouth
defying phonetics
and belonging

every movement of the tongue
accompanied by an indecipherable context

where is that accent from
some mixture of imperialism   d i s l o c a t i o n
privilege
where specifically
on
a
map

an exact location that will help me arrange you

i can offer no simple geographic answer
only that i am trying to make a language mine
this one right here

the one that has colonised vernaculars

wiped-out others

the one with written words that have rescued me
when there was no making sense of the present

Hatchet

Simone Wong

1. The Strike

A hatchet, half-buried in the flaking skin of a gumtree. She is the length of two hands, this axe, and she still trembles from the impact, while the remains of a throat-torn shout weave unendingly between branches, spreading, spreading. Because it is a Sunday, the echoes are ceaseless, with no one to catch them in their ears and to silence with the reductiveness of memory. This is the beginning of her half-life, her body abandoned by virtue of a single splinter. The farmer walks away with a bloody hand.

2. The Engulfing

She succumbs to the bark. It shouts, covers her ears and enfolds her blade (still ringing). Steel once carefully sharpened against black rock now submerges into the thick trunk. A hulk. A prison shelled in wood. But. But sometimes she feels the tree's pulse running, tremoring, down her handle. This prison is canvassed in these thin tendrils of life. It turns her silver into gold.

3. The Knot

It is a gradual thing. It has taken her six years to forget the touch of palms and the soft tips of fingers, ten to realise her body has always been made of wood too. Oh, the smoothness of her ash, particles stacked just as the human body stacks memory beneath skin. The pale gumtree ripples and flakes around the entry point. It puckers. It bubbles. It knots.

4. The Cementation

She breathes with the fluttering heartbeat of the gum. It sighs sometimes, and she is grateful. The knot holds her in like an embrace. She used to see darkness, only black, but now she can see it is a warm colour. Swirls of brown and muted greys, the depths of it beyond her perception. Her head is rusted now, and she does not know, embalmed in the amber. As if a home.

5. The Pull

Lemons. It smells different, like lemons. A certain hot musk that reminds her of summers years ago and long arms shining with perspiration. The citrus is like a sickness, and it leeches into her dusty wood. And then there is a sharp tug, a pressure running deep. When the lemon thing pulls again, she tries to cling, she tries to hold herself within the cocoon of darkness, but she is painfully powerless. Dominated. The walls shatter.

* * *

I pull out my father's hatchet because my mother tells me to. He has been dead for a week now.

The handle is splotchy with marks of mould. Dark ochre climbs up its metal neck and disappears into the peeling bark of the old gum. I give it a few more tugs and it starts to loosen. A sound unties and then unravels from the knot clamping the axe's head – as if an echo chamber reverberating from within.

It is ugly, this detachment. Cracks scale up the trunk, tracing the lines scribbled into its skin. The force of the act shakes dead branches from the forest's gaping roof. A tiny angular stick tumbles down and grazes my sweaty shoulder. I look at the weight in my hands. The axe has refused to give up the wood that has imprisoned it. Patches of dark timber and bits of molten amber streak the once smooth blade. A whorl of browns and oranges, blood red.

The hole it has left in the tree seems like a wound.

I run my hand down the worn handle, perhaps foolishly, and my skin catches on an unperceivable split in the wood. My finger trembles a little, for the shard has buried itself deep within my flesh. I watch as the blood pools, and the splinter is engulfed.

Where I Made You Happy

Chloe Isabelle Pryce

there's another life,
shot through with sepia,
where I taught your kids to swim.
where we bought an apartment out west
and made something wonderful –
or at least made something work.

one fractional shift of the kaleidoscope
to a world in which
you chose me;
where my mum was fairy godmother,
and we held each other skin to skin
in tangles after dark.

so close: my fingertips
meet in the mirror,
you watching from behind.
so close: your son's name
the same as I had
chosen, in secret, for mine.

there is a life, not this one,
where I made you happy.
where we lay the doors wide open,
let the world's strange magic in.
in all my dreaming, I never knew a home
so bewitchingly mundane,
so welcoming and new –

and I rue it,
for we loved each other there.

The Airport

Matilda Meikle

Julie hates weekend traffic. She's on her way to the airport, stuck behind an old woman who's forgotten how to use her indicator and drives twenty below the limit. She watches the clock on her dashboard, anxiety swelling. As usual, she left the house this afternoon with plenty of time to spare, forever nervous about being late, but that doesn't seem to be calming her now.

If her psychologist Dr Patel were here, he'd point out her incessant need to people please as the cause of her distress. Any other day, she'd try one of the breathing exercises he swears by. But unfortunately for her, and her slowly dwindling bank account balance, this is something she'll need more sessions to unpack. Besides, today isn't a normal day. Today, she's picking Grace up from the airport.

Grace, who's been away for the last six months playing soccer at some prestigious college in the UK. Who begged Julie to keep in contact but now seems to be dodging her calls. Which is weird, since Julie and Grace were closer than ever before she left. Julie used to go and watch Grace's soccer matches every Sunday. This was after they'd started sleeping together but before they decided what it actually meant. Somewhere in that no man's land where both girls weren't exactly sure where they stood, or what the other person felt but were still too scared to admit their feelings in case they lost the upper hand of indifference.

Back then, Julie would sit on a cold metal bench, wrapped in a thrift store jumper, and watch as the ball flew up and down the field. Whenever she made eye contact with Grace, she would wave enthusiastically. At most, she would get a nod of acknowledgement. Usually Grace would just ignore her, scared that waving back would somehow implicate her in a lesbian love affair.

Now, as Julie pulls into the arrival bay of the airport, Grace is the one waving passionately on her approach. In one hand she grips the handle of her giant suitcase. In the other, she's holding her phone like a weapon – thrusting it back and forth with each wave, ready to hit a passing tourist.

When Grace first messaged asking for a ride, Julie hadn't known what to expect. Deep down, she'd dreamt of a tear-filled reunion. She wanted to pull Grace against her chest and breath in her fresh smell – a smell that called to her whenever she walked past a field of grass or the outdoor showers at the beach.

She'd hoped, stupidly, that Grace would apologise for the months of silence, and everything would be alright. Instead, words fail them both as Grace loads her bags into the back and climbs into the passenger seat beside Julie.

Not wanting to dwell in silence, perhaps scared of what it says about their changing relationship, Julie places a reassuring hand on Grace's shoulder. Reassuring for who, she can't tell.

"You're here."

"Risen from the dead," Grace replies. She rests her hands on top of Julie's for a moment. And then, pulling back to tuck them behind her head, she sighs.

"Let's get the fuck out of here."

Julie's cue to move. She indicates, checks her blind spot and slips out into the steady flow of traffic.

At first, Grace sits quietly with her eyes closed, light flickering across her face as they drive. Julie begins to worry that the silence will continue. That their time apart has sucked the well of conversation dry. She glances at Grace in her periphery. Looks away. Looks back.

But just as the thoughts begin to consume her, Grace speaks. The rising bubble of panic surrounding Julie bursts, the mist settling back into her skin.

"I missed you Jules," Grace starts, turning her head so she can look at Julie's profile. "English girls don't get me like you do."

She doesn't elaborate. She doesn't have to. Julie knows Grace still thinks about those nights, just like she does. They feel deeply private, almost secret.

Grace was the first person Julie told about her depression. At the time, she'd simply reached out to take Julie's hand in her own, rubbing her thumb up and down in a soothing pattern. Julie felt more attracted to Grace in that moment than when they'd first seen each other naked. Their souls had connected.

She didn't like to think about Grace sharing those same moments with other girls. English girls.

"So, have you made any friends?" she asks.

"Sure, lots. People seem to like me more over there. I think it's my accent."

Julie feels Grace smirk rather than seeing it. She's keeping her eyes locked on the road, not wanting to give herself away. Needing to discover where Grace stands before revealing her own cards. Although she doubts it's making a difference. Grace has always had this power over her. It used to be charming. Today, it's just annoying.

"No need to stress Jules. You're still my favourite."

As close to an apology as Julie is going to get. A car honks from somewhere behind them.

"What've I missed?"

Grace knows she's been a bad friend, but still expects to pick up where they left off. And Julie kicks herself, because of course she wants the same. After all, Grace was Julie's first love.

Julie was Grace's first girlfriend. They weren't the same thing.

Overcome with energy, Julie begins kneading the steering wheel between her palms. Shrugs. Grace doesn't relent.

"Come on," she teases, placing a warm hand on Julie's leg. "There's gotta be something. Besides pining after me, obviously."

Julie can't help the flare in her nostrils. Suddenly, she's overcome by the urge to hurt Grace. She wants Grace to feel the same way she does every time a call goes to voicemail, or a text sits unanswered for days. Her mouth starts moving before her brain has caught up.

"I'm seeing someone."

Silence. The hollow growl of wheels on the road.

Grace nods, removes her hand from Julie's leg. They pull up at a set of traffic lights and Julie watches as a man in the grey ute beside them fiddles with his rearview mirror. Car engines rev. They start moving again.

"Who?"

Grace tries too hard to sound casual. Just like her to assume she's the only one who can move on.

"His name is Andrew."

"Andrew." Grace rolls the name around in her mouth. Decides it's sour. Spits it back out. "Andrew? As in . . . a man?"

Ah, there it is.

"Yeah."

Grace laughs. Actually barks. The sound doesn't suit her. "But you're gay?"

She phrases it like a question, but it's so much more than that.

And it's true – Julie never imagined being with a guy after she met Grace. The online quizzes and late nights flicking between pictures of male and female celebrities to determine whether her stomach really somersaulted had told her just as much. Besides, there was no way anything would compare to the way she felt when they were together . . . until Andrew showed up in her seminar. This tall, hazel boy who smelt of vanilla. Who asked questions and remembered things she said. Suddenly, Julie began to wonder if her attraction had more to do with the person than the gender. When Andrew finally worked up the courage to ask her out, after weeks of texting back and forth, she'd been curious to explore what it felt like.

And, for the most part, it felt good. He came over just to chat about their boring days and didn't mind when she held his hand in public. He was dependable, steady. Everything Grace wasn't.

And yet . . . if she was being honest, Julie liked Andrew the most when she was alone in her dorm room at night. When the quiet grew too loud and he was only a phone call away. It might not be passionate, he might snore and take her to movies she had no interest in, but she was content. Right?

The revelation of Julie's expanding life seems to shock Grace more than expected.

"Umm, okay."

And then:

"You'll have to introduce me."

Julie nods, but she has no intention of letting them meet. Grace would eat Andrew alive. The thought makes her smile, and then immediately prickle with guilt.

They're getting close to the house now, minutes ticking down. Julie can tell because they pass the old kebab joint the girls used to frequent after a long night out. Grace straightens up, folding her hands across her chest.

"So, what, you're into dick all of a sudden?"

"Come on."

"No, I'm serious. What changed?"

The self-righteousness in Grace's stare ignites Julie's anger once again.

"You left."

Her calm tone surprises both of them.

"We don't really talk anymore, do we?"

The words hang heavy in the air. Julie turns off the highway and onto suburban streets as she waits for a response. A sign advertises charming family-sized condos close to good schools.

"Look, I –"

Grace clenches her jaw, dropping her shoulders like the strings keeping her together have finally been cut.

"It's been lonely, you know?" Julie picks at her eyebrow as Grace speaks. They've both been lonely. "I understand if you hate me."

"I don't hate you." Julie's response is instant. A reflex.

"Actually, I can't hate you."

Ironic, she thinks. No matter what Grace does or how many times she lets Julie down, the answer will always be the same.

Julie can't help the tug at her chest. The need to reach for Grace across the long months apart.

She looks over for the first time, their eyes catching as she asks a silent question – is this real? Grace replies without saying a word. Of course.

"I really have missed you, Jules."

It's all Julie needs. She breathes in, letting her frustration go with the air from her lungs.

As if on cue, they turn onto Grace's street. When they pull up in front of the house, Julie watches Grace play with the handle of the door.

"I'll see you around then?" she asks, not meeting Julie's gaze.

"Yeah, I'll call you."

She will. They both know she will.

Tina and the Old Man

Sharmila Jayasinghe

The old man who lived oceans away had been a non-existent entity in Tina's life for the entire time she knew her soon-to-be husband. He was the sort of person who was mentioned in passing sometimes and forgotten most of the time. The sort who certainly was never expected to visit. But that all changed when Tina's soon-to-be husband announced the impending arrival of his father.

"Thaththa will come a few weeks early. You and he can bond." Hearing those words, Tina nearly fell off her perch on the bar stool in the kitchen of their small apartment.

Tina was fatherless and didn't want to inherit a father. She sighed. "So, he finally decided to come?" she asked, controlling her tone.

"I made the decision. Not him." The husband-to-be was eager, his tone one of triumph.

Tina had grown quite accustomed to her husband-to-be's convenient "orphaned" status. With his father oceans away, Tina had always felt a sense of relief. The situation suited her just fine. After all, dealing with her own overbearing mother was enough of a challenge; she certainly didn't need another parent orbiting their space and adding to her stress. Her husband-to-be's unique family dynamic was a godsend – just one parent, conveniently located overseas, and no impending visits to disrupt their blissful bubble. Tina couldn't bear the thought of this ideal situation being shattered.

So when the impending arrival was announced, Tina felt like a snowman in a heatwave – melting with anxiety and dripping with worry.

"You made the decision." She repeated her husband-to-be's words as a statement, not a question. She peered into his face, trying to gauge his excitement against her non-excitement.

The days leading up to the arrival were uneventful. The husband-to-be pottered around like nothing important was happening.

Tina sulked, secretly.

When the day of the arrival arrived, Tina had no choice but to accompany her soon-to-be husband to the airport. Excuses had churned in her mind: a pretend asthma attack, stomach flu, an office meeting. But the excuses had stayed as mere thoughts and hadn't materialised as words.

The old man bounced out to the waiting bay at the airport with a trolly full of suitcases like it was not a temporary visit but a permanency. Tina clenched her teeth so as not to let her jaw fall. Her mind immediately registered an other-worldliness about the man. He was very brown, like he had been standing in a paddy field in the blazing sun all his life. He was short, like a hobbit, and waddled in overly large socks and sandal-covered feet. His hair was unruly and grey, haloing a perfect melon-shaped head. He wore thick-rimmed glasses which added to his alienness. His attire was a mash-up: a red and black flannel shirt under a dated tweed coat in a mustard shade, and long dirty green pants that fell below his ankles.

Tina's nose wrinkled like an un-ironed handkerchief when the old man stopped near and imbued her space with the reek of the eleven-hour plane ride. She greeted him with a curt nod, skipping the formalities of cheek-kissing or handshaking. To her surprise, the old man didn't scrutinise her. Instead, he offered a warm smile and lowered his head. Tina straightened her back and assumed a superior stance. Her husband-to-be stood by, speechless, with a tear in his eye. He reached the old man eagerly, greeting him with gestures bordering on reverence, as though he were meeting a deity.

Tina's mind was too busy critiquing to feel emotional.

The old man did not, by any means, have a towering personality, but as soon as he stepped into their home, Tina sensed the surroundings bowing down to him. Without skipping a beat, he commandeered Tina's kitchen, conjuring up pots of oil-drenched, spice-infused dishes that Tina's husband-to-be devoured with gusto, leaving no morsel behind. He licked his fingers with such enthusiasm that Tina couldn't help but wonder, "Didn't I cook dal and chicken curry the way he instructed? Wasn't that good enough?" From then on, Tina's mind became a torture chamber of culinary self doubt.

When Tina vented to her mother, expecting sympathy, she was met with anything but.

"He's a cook in a hotel after all, right? So, what's the problem? Let the man cook!" her mother said, as if Tina had attempted to restrict a Michelin-starred chef from accessing her kitchen.

"It's good to get some culture into you!" her mother added with a chuckle, clearly amused by Tina's struggles.

And if that wasn't enough, her friend chimed in, "I would give an arm and a leg for someone to cook me every meal!" Tina couldn't help but roll her eyes. It seemed like everyone was suddenly a fan of the old man; everyone but her.

The cooking show continued morning, noon and night: the father cooking, the son gorging. As the alien aromas clung to every surface like a persistent house guest, Tina couldn't help but unleash her arsenal of Dusk candles, waging a fragrant war to reclaim her space.

As the days progressed, Tina couldn't believe the transformation of her husband-to-be; the "old man invasion" turned him into a live wire, buzzing around the house like a hyperactive teen on caffeine. Gone was the reserved guy she knew, replaced by a giggling chatterbox marvelling at every bizarre gift bestowed upon him by his father, from creepy wooden devil masks that screamed Halloween to elephants with trunks held high in a defiant stance against good taste to coconut spoons that seemed better suited for a witch's brew than breakfast cereal. The fact that he had taken an unheard of break from work to lounge around the house in a sarong and a banian, an outfit combo previously reserved for beach vacations, baffled Tina further.

Tina's disappointment at the new world around her knew no end. The invasion of the Orient continued, and before she knew it, her once muted home became a cultural carnival, with artifacts splashed about like confetti after a particularly enthusiastic wedding. A life-sized elephant statue stood guard at the entrance to their apartment, its trunk held high in a greeting that Tina felt screamed, "Welcome to the jungle!" A small army of miniature gods took up residence in a corner of the study surrounding a six-inch white-washed Buddha. Incense and camphor secured from the streets of Toongabbie burnt afoot the gaudy display. The television blared out ethnic tunes day in and day out, with women in sarees twirling around trees in the rain on the screen. Multicoloured sarongs and white banians staged a coup on the clothes rack, overthrowing Tina's delicates.

As the collision of cultures turned her home into a Bollywood set, Tina felt like an extra relegated to the background, popping up only when absolutely necessary – cue the awkward smile and the fake warmth.

The old man and Tina's husband-to-be were having a grand old time, bonding over memories and quirky trinkets like a couple of long lost buddies reunited at Parklea markets. Tina couldn't join in the father-son banter that flowed effortlessly in a language she'd never learnt, nor could she stomach the never ending parade of spice-laden dishes cluttering up her kitchen counter. Feeling abandoned and bewildered, she couldn't help but wonder, "How can an invited guest take over the house like this?"

In her quest for sympathy, Tina turned to her mother again. But instead of solace, she got a dose of brutal honesty. "Reverse colonisation," her mother quipped, dismissing Tina's complaints with a single, cutting phrase.

Just when she thought things couldn't get any worse, the dreaded day arrived when her husband-to-be had to return to work, leaving her alone with the old man. Tina resigned herself to this fate, retreating to her bedroom and pacing endlessly, emerging only when absolutely necessary.

A moment of respite descended upon Tina like a gift from the universe: a golden opportunity to sneak out onto the balcony for a much needed cigarette. But as Tina basked in the clandestine pleasure of her smoke break, the old man appeared like a spectre in the mist, a silent guardian of the balcony, ready to extinguish any flicker of rebellion. Tina's heart somersaulted into her stomach as she spun around, attempting to conceal the incriminating evidence, feeling like one of her students, or a high school delinquent caught red-handed in the principal's office. The old man leaned against the half wall, a mischievous grin dancing on his lips, thoroughly entertained by Tina's clumsy antics. Then, with a theatrical flourish and a nod worthy of a silent movie star, he extended his hand, silently requesting a puff. Tina's eyebrows shot up in surprise, but her relief was palpable as they stood side by side, sharing a smoke-filled moment. It was in that shared cloud of nicotine and camaraderie that Tina's eyes opened to a startling revelation that the old man was just as stressed as she was about the situation they were in.

Tina cursed her own non-bilingualism while the balcony morphed into a truce zone, a sanctuary where the old man and Tina escaped the chaos of their minds and sought solace in a shared understanding.

Later that day, Tina was pulling on an oversized jumper and her fiancé's long track pants when the old man knocked on her bedroom door. The old man greeted her with a mug of some aromatic concoction. No words were shared as the steaming mug was passed from the old man to Tina. The pair made hopeful gestures at each other, Tina bowing in acknowledgment the same way the ladies at the sushi train bowed after receiving payment, the old man raising his hand in a half salute, unsure what his proper reaction should be. The postures of cultural confusion ended as quickly as they had begun and the old man marched away to the kitchen. Tina followed, mug in hand. Standing in the corridor, she watched the old man's activity discreetly. The old man perched himself on a wooden stool and started scribbling in a small notebook. His eyes remained glued to the page, but at intervals, his hand stopped writing. Lost in a thought, he let his finger click on the ballpoint pen incessantly.

Tina wondered what he might be writing. Recipes? Maybe a shopping list? Gifts to take for his many relatives when he returned home? Or maybe a to-do list? His son was known to do that. Or could it be his will? He was, after all, fragile and sickly and was acting like he wanted to go. Tina felt ashamed of her last thought and attempted to brush it off. Her mind was a haze. She didn't know what to think of the old man now. Not after the smoke-filled episode they'd shared on the balcony. Tina felt a warmth she had never felt before and smiled to herself, but instead of joining the old man at the bench, she slid the glass door open quietly and stepped outside. Her eyes didn't want to leave the scribbling old man as she eased herself onto a rattan chair and let the aromatic concoction serenade her insides. The old man continued scribbling, lost in his world. He seemed vulnerable and in need of being taken care of.

Pulling the hoodie over her head to shield herself from a sudden gush of cold wind, she pushed the sliding door shut with her foot to stop the chilly air from waltzing in and menacing the old man on the bar stool.

Chrysanthemums

Natalie Susak

After we land / we go / to white chrysanthemum / funerals /
    where you remember
your father / his moss-covered grave / leaving the hotel you
    search for him / dawn
still curling / around the edges / of a too-long night / the body
    is only a body / until
it is a thing / laid heavy on a table / it is amazing how matter /
    changes / how rain turns
to sleet / while two women in a graveyard / learn to pray / how
    your ink blot hair /
cuts through morning fog / clean as a knife / In Hrvatski I do
    not know the word
for apple / or knife / or how to find the gap / between loss and
    longitude / how about
loss / and longing? / At the dinner table / I am the mute girl /
    the ghost crushing /
white chrysanthemums on the lawn / I only call myself
    Hrvatica in the online form /
where I change my surname / to yours.

Con, Ma

Johnny Banh

She didn't know what the word was in English. How to say the worst part about being alone.

Mai could feel their cold presence, hovering outside the bungalow windows. If she leaned in and pressed her cheeks against the glass, she could hear them murmuring. Her Vietnamese-English dictionary gave her a translation: ma(n): ghost. But it was wrong. For one, nouns are objects. People, places, things. Miss Pennisi had taught the class about nouns, earlier that week. She had them repeat it back to her in unison. People, places, things. People, places, things. The ma wasn't really any of these. And secondly, ghosts were not real.

The ma was real, and she'd known this since she was five. There was an old lady who lived down the road, back in her hometown. She had fashioned herself a hut in between the local bar and a hotel, scrapping together walls, which were held together with mud and beaten down on by the sun. The pale straw roof crumpled at the edges, aching from the years of monsoon dripping down the roof. No one spoke to her. No one spoke about her. That was the silent agreement amongst the neighbourhood, something Mai noticed even as a child. It was held in a hurried pace past her hut, an avoidant gaze up towards the sky, or sometimes, in eyes staring in fiery condemnation. Mai didn't know her name. All the adults just called her bụi đời (n): life dust.

Even the kids picked up on this exclusion too. The boys turned it into a game of who could get the closest to the old lady's house without getting caught. Mai sat with the girls, and they instead spread rumours about the bụi đời. She remembered how close-knit the group was, meeting every morning on the streetside curb to chat, even doing their hair the same way to signify their friendship. All the girls curled their hair at the tips with pencils and rubber bands, an attempt to mirror those American beauties in the cinema downtown. Their conversations echoed down the busy street, hovering over the bustle of the markets. The bụi đời fascinated the group, and every week they would propose new theories on the old lady. One of them heard from her parent's uncle's sister that the bụi đời was actually a man. Another whispered that the bụi đời was a spy sent by America to find Bác Hồ. Maybe she was an illegal immigrant from Japan. Maybe she'd had an affair with a government official.

Mai knew they were all making up stories, seeing who could create the most outrageous one. Her mother told her the truth. Bụi đời là người má: The life dust is a mother. She had said it so casually, words spoken over the steam rising out of a pot. Mà con ma trắng ăn cắp em bé: But the white ghosts took her baby away.

At first, Mai thought she was trying to scare her. Or maybe she was making one of those jokes only adults understand. But it bothered her for the rest of the night, those words settling into the pit of her stomach. In the morning, when she passed the bụi đời's house, she peered through a crack in the planks and saw it in the darkness. A makeshift crib, covered by a baby blanket. It was true, these ghosts took babies.

Where was her baby?

For a brief moment, Mai felt panic seizing her throat. She looked out onto the street through the window. Did she leave the baby in the pram? She found herself unlocking the front door, racing across the veranda, down the creaking steps screeching out at her as the streetlights cast long shadows chasing her feet, pounding the grass lawn. But the pram was empty. And she didn't know how she would explain it to the police. She didn't even know how to call the police. And her husband wouldn't be home for a few more hours. And everyone she knew was on a different continent. And she knew the ma was laughing at her.

Her baby was fast asleep in the cot. Safe. Sleeping soundly in front of the television.

Mai let out a long sigh, before she looked out the window again. Her husband wouldn't be back from work for another hour. She really shouldn't call him her baby anymore. He was three now. A toddler, almost a young child, not a baby. It was strange though, calling him a toddler. He would always be her em bé, her baby. Finding her dictionary, Mai began thumbing through her pages, looking for the word toddler. She had placed a sticky note on that page a few months ago, a yellowed reminder of important words to remember: toddler (n): đứa bé chỉ mới biết đi. There wasn't even a word for toddler in Vietnamese. Just a clumsy approximation. Her baby was apparently a child who just started walking. It wasn't true though, since her baby was walking at an extremely early age. Even the doctor was a little surprised, especially at the fact that he was already crawling at six months old. By the next checkup, he could basically walk around the entire doctor's office, only stumbling a few times. Her baby was a toddler in less than a year. Impossible.

She noticed a white scrap of paper hanging off the corner of the dictionary and flicked over to the page to reattach it: autism (n): bệnh tự kỷ. This one was recent. She'd tried to look for this definition a couple of weeks ago. The preschool teacher had pulled Mai aside as she was picking up her baby. Normally the teacher was the bubbly type, smiling and beaming at the children. But on this day, her words were flatly whispered, too quiet for Mai to even try to understand what she was saying. The teacher handed her a letter and a business card, which, when Mai asked her husband later that day, led her to a specialist's office on the outskirts of town. As her baby explored the stuffy office, carefully examining the various certificates pinned on the greying blue walls, the doctor explained the teacher's concerns. How she was worried that her baby didn't fit in, and didn't make friends. How he played alone. How he didn't seem to understand instructions. How he always refused to participate in finger painting, and how writing was an impossible task.

Although Mai didn't want to admit it, she hated writing too. For one, holding a pen hurt her hands. Sitting at her desk, she'd curled in her fingers into a fist around the pen's body, pressing into it until her knuckles turned white, and her fingertips red. And despite that, her words seemed to trail off the line, lighter and lighter till the ink fell off the page. She admired how her classmate, a young girl from India who was maybe twenty years old, could do it so naturally and without any breaks. Mai tried to copy her one time, the way she held the pen. Her long and smooth fingers effortlessly wrapped around the pencil and seemed to glide across the page. Mai quickly gave up. Miss Pennisi was not subtle with her praise for the girl's handwriting. Exemplar. Outstanding.

Remarkable. Mai always made a note of these in her dictionary after class.

And she did not trust words. Written words, anyways. They were so easy to change, to fake, to forge. She knew first-hand, thinking back to the identity cards back home. Words were lifeless and silent, bodies dragged out of the pen barrel. Every mark made is vulnerable, to the smudge of hand, a scribble across the word. And the paper itself? Burnt, torn, crumpled, trashed. Given time, all things turn to dust, and words were no different. But when you speak, the words are truly yours. Once spoken, they cannot be returned. They could not be caught at their throats with the point of a pen. Not like written words.

Mai knew that only spoken words were alive. Her teacher's words danced across the fluorescent bulbs as she exaggerated her lips, her teeth for all to copy that perfect pronunciation every student in that room dreamed of. Mai's husband spoke English in a rush of stilted words, his tongue barely holding onto each vowel as he attempted to collect them into words. When her baby babbled to her, she watched that jumble of sounds escape his gummy mouth, stumbling and scattering themselves onto the tile floor. But his words weren't always random. Mai noticed a pattern to his speech. If she sat in front of him, held both of his hands, and repeated a syllable over and over, he would do his best to copy her. Sometimes she would catch him afterwards in his playpen, still trying to mimic her voice as he lined up his toy cars. His voice floated up above him, filling the room with consonants and vowels.

She did her best to teach him what she knew. All useful things, of course. Numbers. Shapes. How to ask for directions. How to greet someone. How to apologise. But only in English. There was a time, when he was a year old, when Mai tried to teach him Vietnamese. It was only a dream, but one day, she'd want the two of them to go home, where she could show him the streets where she grew up. Underneath her clothes in the closet, she stashed away a box of change, three to four notes from her husband's pockets, coins left on pavements. And every day, she tried to get her baby to say má (n): mother; mum. He almost had it, after a few months. Mà and mả and mạ and mã darted out of his mouth, hidden among his gibberish. But not má. The tone was never quite right. Her husband caught her soon after, when he came home from work early. "There's no need for Vietnamese here in Australia," he sternly said. "My son will be Australian."

Her baby woke up, startled. Ten more minutes till her husband came home.

Looking out the window, she wondered whether the ma was still there. But she wasn't worried about them anymore. She'd have to warm up dinner and finish dusting the house soon. Mai carried him out of his crib and lifted him onto the living room floor. As she watched him walk over to his toy cars, she felt a warmth filling her body. Admittedly, she did think about it at times, if he would ever fit in. Soon he would be in primary school, and she wouldn't be there for him. Would he ever fit in? Would he belong?

But he will grow up fine, she told herself, and he will fit right in when he's older. Nothing to worry about. She tried beckoning him to her. "Come to má." Má. Má. Má. Má.

But all that came out of her baby was ma.

Ma, ma, ma, ma.

The Inferno of the Living

Joe Denman

Phonetics

Say the word "belonging";
feel the sensation of an idea
roll through the soft flesh of your mouth
like a child entering a new world.

It begins at a bridge between
an outside and an interior,
boldly questioning the liminality
of one and many.
The thirty-two white pearls
cradle the bilabial beginning,
quietly whispering that the world –
yes, your small, beautiful world
is nothing but an oyster.

Feel the idea float to the palate;
it teeters between the first and the last –
a sigh that opens the future
from one to many and lifts the
tongue to the roof of a cavern.
It is here, in this long, infinite

corridor that the idea draws towards
a collective, or at least
the idea of a collective.

Listen as the sonics wend into
an ending encompassing the many
like a fence building itself around the universe.
Feel the language cradle the uvula
and enter the audio of nasality;
a sound beginning in the collective,
a vibration signalling to the soul
that it can remain.
Step back from your body, your voice
and see the power of a beginning.
A beginning grips the centre of a story
as a garden path wanders from a doorway.
To begin we must speak.
But before speaking, before anything,
we must belong.

A Road to Genesis

I would like to build something out of fragments of nothing.

We begin in a place that holds us as a budding flower holds its destiny. A place where we all begin, a pin on the border of a map. Its scale reads *water quenches fire*. We begin as a tear drop that is purely fixated on the future. Our past is as empty as a dry creek-bed, our future as endless as the crashing of waves.

Now enter.

Take note of the darkness, the moisture, the warmth. We watch ourselves and see how our soul is woven from the loose ends of the universe. The womb is a vast place. It is a place so utterly beautiful.

Beginnings often are.

A beginning is the pure and effortless part of a story, perhaps the only one. The tale that follows is long and arduous, riddled with the vulgarities of life on earth. An inferno that we do not yet know pulls at our borders like a child tugging on a father's pant leg. For months we are nothing more than a globule of flesh that portends the creation of conscience. We are ensconced within the womb, tentatively wending our appendages through viscous fluid, pushing the boundaries of our newfound nest. As the neurons in our brain mature, a wordless thought echoes in this seemingly indefinite and endless chamber – *home*. How can home be where the heart is when the heart is an unfinished entity?

We are suddenly too large for this place, the only place we have ever known. It is not our choice to leave; we are wrenched from the womb as a wren plucks a worm from the earth. Birth is always a painful sentence. To belong to this world, we put a woman through a furnace.

We are pulled, screaming, from *home* into a world that is so utterly full it is asking for us to leave, and yet a place that we must call *home*. We begin with a sound that draws a line between us. We turn our heads and ball our fists as the truths of this world are thrust upon us. We begin, as we end, belonging to an inferno.

Nacre of Syllables

There are an infinite number of things
we do not belong to.
That is why what we do belong to
is so important.
As precious as a pearl.

The world is your oyster
so open up
see
feel
think
hear
say the word "belonging"

The thirty-two pearls hold a bilabial beginning
to be.
The inferno of the living is not something that will be.

The long, empty corridor stands in between:
to long.
Become such a part of the inferno that you can no longer
see it.

The small nasality of a gerund suffix expands the syntax:
to endure.
Separate what is the pearl from what is the inferno;
make it endure, give it space.

Listen,
We were

We are
We will be.

Proprioception

Vanessa Yenson

Proprioception

/prəʊprɪəˈsɛpʃn/
The ability to ascertain the position of one's body in
space without the need for visual cues.
— Definition from memory of university notes 1995

Proprioception. I learnt this word in my first year at university
studying speech pathology. It piled high among new medical
words with deep roots in classical languages; anatomical words
that flowed off the tongues of my friends who studied biology
or Latin at school. I had studied physics and chemistry, like my
siblings.
Proprioception.
I roll this word around my brain as I feel my body on the
Reformer Pilates bed. My back is supported by the carriage,
my head rests between the shoulder blocks and there is a
tugging as my feet in the straps pull down on the ropes.
I close my eyes, focusing on the physical sensations as my
straight legs rise slowly together, hamstrings stretching; the
carriage inches forward beneath me, the springs eager to close;
I feel my inner thighs strain as I split my legs apart, muscles

shaking imperceptibly; hips roll in their joints, contracting and elongating old muscles as I circle my legs.

Proprioception. The awareness of the position and movement of the body.

I marvel that my brain can track every part of my body in space without looking; that I can control motion, speed, direction and stretch just by thought; that I can sense the deliberate movement of the carriage back and forth along the metal rails because the endolymph brushes the hair cells lining my balance organ. When I was a child, I enjoyed closing my eyes on the swing – without the visual cues, the constant change in direction was too fast for the endolymph to establish if I was moving forward or backward, up or down, making me feel discombobulated, like I was hovering or not really there at all.

As I circle my legs in the opposite direction, I start to wonder if there is an equivalent concept to describe the cognisance of where each of us is in the journey of our own lives, if we are aware of the conscious and subconscious control of our decisions or external factors that intercept our path and change our trajectory through life.

As the youngest of four, I have always had a strong sense of place and purpose. Before my earliest memories, we lived with my Chinese ex-pat grandparents on a little estate in Essexwold, Johannesburg. Combined with yellowing photographs, the stories told and retold by parents and siblings have created a nest of images and emotions so real that I can almost reach through time and reality, feel the texture and breathe the air.

I sit on a blanket in dappled shade in the garden, surrounded by red and orange leaves; Dad clicks the camera as I study one with infantile intensity, twirling the stem between my fingers before raising it to my mouth to take a bite. My brothers zoom around the house on their bikes, using the sides of their shoes to brake in a plume of dust. Townsend, our gardener, watches them with his big smile, impossibly white teeth flashing from beneath the shadow of his hat and dark skin. He gives my eldest brother a high five at the win and, with a deep chuckle, returns to his chores. My sister, perhaps at a ballet lesson, returns to join them to climb the mulberry tree. I watch them from below, listening to their chatter, longing to be a part of their world. My heart soars to the branches above; I can almost taste the sweetness as the juices dribble down my imagination. They descend with stained hands, chins and cheeks, unable to deny their antics. I toddle after them as they scamper into the house, careful not to scuff the floors that Dora has just polished.

On her wedding day, my mother's intricate hairdo epitomised 1960s glamour with its style, sheen and height. In the black and white photos, I see a stunningly beautiful young woman half my current age, whose childhood and adolescence I will never truly know. She is a stranger, her youthful energy and excitement captured in time. And yet I see these same emotions on each of my friends' faces on their own wedding days – young women with hopes and dreams standing at an altar vowing to love and honour a man for the rest of their lives. Could Mum sense her journey, the proprioception of her life? The world was changing all around them – South Africa's apartheid was stretching like a rubber band, threatening to snap in two or fling off into the distance, whole and resilient. My family did not fit in as white or black – we were an in-between race who contributed to society without really being seen or valued. As Dad slid the ring on her finger, no crystal ball could have predicted that they would emigrate halfway around the world to Australia twelve years later with four kids in tow. Being two years old, I ran up and down the aisles of the plane, waddling in my childish bliss and bulky cloth nappy.

* * *

Proprioception. The awareness of control over your physical being and the sensory feedback that confirms your existence.

In Sydney, my strong sense of self and place in the world continued along an expected path. I never cried if I lost sight of Mum or Dad when the family went late-night shopping; after all, I knew where I was. I idolised my siblings – I traipsed after them, wanting to be seen, to be included. The four, six and nine year age gaps seemed like chasms too wide to cross.

I sit on the ground by the burnt orange corduroy couch, watching my brothers assemble Lego, turning green, blue and red blocks into the shapes of sturdy pistols. I watch as they start their spy hunt, stalking each other around the house, slinking up to corners and taking imaginary shots. Pew! Pew! I glance down at a Donald Duck jigsaw puzzle I have assembled many times before; now the scattered pieces have lost their appeal. I can hear scales and arpeggios echoing from the piano in the study, my sister's diligent fingers running through their daily practice, getting faster and more precise with each iteration. Mum calls them to do their homework, and I race ahead, pulling out my colouring books and pencils to join in; they glance at me sideways and shake their heads.

One of my earliest ambitions was to be a mother. A mother, just like mine, with two boys and two girls.

After dinner, while the dishes are being washed, dried and put away, I haul out the barrel vacuum to clean under the table and by the legs of those washing up. Dad points – I am so small, I fit under the kitchen bench as I work – but I cannot hear their laughter over the roar of the vacuum.

My other childish goal was to be a patient so I could see more of my father, who worked long hours establishing his medical practice in a very white part of Sydney. As I grew, I did not see the physical differences between our family and those around us in the Sutherland Shire and St George area. My parents spoke fluent English and Afrikaans, but the Cantonese and Hakka dialect that my grandparents spoke were left behind in Johannesburg as if we couldn't pack them in with our furniture and belongings. Dad spent long hours at work, visiting nursing homes and making house calls. We would wait for his canary-yellow Datsun to rumble into the driveway positioning ourselves to yell "FIRST!" and be the lucky one to give him the welcoming hug and kiss.

On the days I wasn't at preschool, I accompanied Mum to the surgery where she worked as a receptionist.

I am sitting on the red plastic children's table in the corner of the waiting room, drawing a square house with two windows, a front door, and a chimney. I am adding in the stick figure family when a lady walks in, hands Mum her Medicare card and sits on the padded black bench beside me.

"You're old," I say. She has a stiff blue bouffant perm, thickly applied foundation and bright red lipstick that bleeds into the wrinkles around her mouth. The room is quiet except for Mum's sharp intake of breath.

"Why do you say that, dear?" Her expression is unreadable. I turn back to my drawing.

"Because you're older than me!"

Across the room, I hear Mum exhale.

* * *

Vertigo

/vɜtəgoʊ/
Sense of dizziness often caused by disturbance of the vestibular system, which is essential for balance.
– Definition from memory of university notes
1995–1997

As a child, I didn't realise that some wishes do come true. In my third year at university, I was diagnosed with acute lymphoblastic leukaemia and became a patient. I was twenty years old, teetering on the cusp of independence and in the blink of a lymph node removal and bone marrow biopsy, I lost my bearings – I was the little child once more, eyes shut tight on the swing, feeling ungrounded, unsure and very, very disoriented.

"Where am I?" The room is smaller than yesterday. And brighter. Yesterday feels like an age ago, as if I am looking back through time down a long kaleidoscope that cannot focus – hazy around the edges – images and memories morphing into each other. Multicoloured get well cards are pinned on the wall and a line of beady-eyed teddy bears watch me from the windowsill. "Who am I?"

Mum's eyebrows furrow.

"I am Rebecca!" The name surfaces from the depths, muddled with dreams of a silver horse that I declare needs to be fed.

By the time my eldest brother arrives for his daily visit, Mum has convinced me that I am not Rebecca, nor have I ever owned any pets, large or small.

"Let's write down what you do remember," he suggests, gently taking the pen from me. My hands tremble and I am not sure if it is from confusion or the high doses of corticosteroids pulsing through my body.

My voice is small as I list the snippets that flash in the fog of my memory, like scenes on the circular disc of photographs in the old View-Master toy:

CLICK

Listening to another lady on the ward having a bone marrow biopsy, her moans of pain behind closed curtains fuelling my own anxiety.

CLICK

Waking in the morning to see her peering at me on the way to the bathroom, her voice quietly marvelling that I look like a sleeping angel with a halo of black hair.

CLICK

Friends sitting by my bed as I curl over a green kidney-shaped bowl, vomiting over and over, while Janet in the bed behind them presses her call button, yelling for help.

CLICK

Watching a young nurse joke with Janet on the way to the shower, oxygen tank tucked behind the wheelchair.

CLICK

The agitation crawling under my skin as the side effects from the corticosteroids and strong chemotherapy break through the prophylactic sedatives.

CLICK

Looking up at another nurse as they wheel my bed into my own single room, wondering if I will ever see Janet again.

* * *

Nystagmus

/nɪsˈtægməs/

The fast, reflexive movement of the eyeballs side-to-side that occurs after sudden changes in direction.

– Definition from memory of university notes 1995–1997 and university experiment observing someone's eyes as they opened them after being spun in a chair blindfolded.

I have drifted in the months and years since – my sense of proprioception in a constant state of flux – resuming studies only to relapse thirteen months later, desperately seeking a compatible bone marrow donor, receiving stem cells from the umbilical cord of a baby born the year I was diagnosed. I have fallen into different university degrees, different opportunities, different interests. My path has not intersected with love or a family of my own. I am the fun aunt, the friend who never forgets Christmas cards, the one whose smile camouflages an overwhelming sense of self-loathing and survivor guilt. Every day is circular. I exercise and build strength, only to catch a cold I cannot shake and struggle to regain wasted muscle. I sign up to dating apps, only to meet guys who aren't ready for anything serious.

As the Pilates class finishes, I think back to the confident little girl I once was – her world reliable, her steps unfaltering and fearless. I picture her on the swing, eyes closed, legs pumping, head thrown back in joy. She looks up at me, jumps off the swing and slips her small hand in mine.

"Come on," she says. "Let's go."

I Came Fleeting on a Boat
Soralinn

I was seventeen when I was told to get out of there – where it
was all of me, *who I knew.*
All of the you.

Alone – I counted up the seventeenth finger. I cut them all off
and cast 'em far.
Making room for numbers to fold away later.
I hated red. I hated blood.
Water, red in my home, you could not open your eyes
underneath.
Everyone drowned.
You cannot see. I dare you. Try.

I was shoved, sat in a single-seater boat.
I was pushed by those who swam in the depth-less pool.
"Go now," I promised the pinkie finger, I couldn't see because
she was too far – drowning in the blood of her dear.
"I will run far, I will come back with a boat that fits all you
lot."

Red unerasing, only then I knew.
With all those fingers hacked.

My memories above the land,
I didn't know the way to row.

The Tense Discourse

Eeshita

Like a family after an argument, we are at the dining table, annoyed, yet unable to get up and walk away. The chandelier casts an eerie glow over the glass-topped dark wood. I sit at the head chair with all my time laid out around me – the Past sitting to the left and the Future occupying the right. The left side of the table is the most alive with flickering flashes of memories and familiar voices. It single-handedly keeps up the conversation.

"Remember that one time you almost started a book club with the neighbourhood kids? You had everything planned. It would've worked out fine, had any of them been a reader! You forgot to take that into account, didn't you?"

I wasn't sure if I wanted it to stop talking or to keep going, for I liked the image that it was conjuring up from the folds of time. That girl, she sounds fun, but I wonder what she'd think of me if we ever met. The Past doesn't seem to notice how I squirm in my seat. I doubt it cares how I feel, it simply goes on like a Shakespearean monologue.

I turn sideways and a chill runs down my spine. The Future is a shadowed being, I can't really make out where it starts or ends, just that it occupies a place on this table. Always so silent, I wonder if it even has a voice. There was a time when I tried to make a conversation:

"So . . ." I started hesitantly, "how's it going over there?"
Static.

"Alright then."

Maybe it is better this way, because who knows what the Future holds or what it might reveal. What if it isn't something I can handle? What if it's everything I've ever been afraid of? What if I am better not knowing?

I sigh and end up staring straight ahead. There, on the seat directly opposite mine, the Present smirks. He leans forward with hands clasped on the table. Instinctively, I look away but I can feel his eyes on me. Why won't he stop staring? Every time I catch a glimpse of him, the amused expression unnerves me. What is so interesting? I ignore him as much as I can, but that doesn't seem to matter. He looks at me as if I were an unpredictable lab experiment and he was making a progress report. Noting my inclination towards the Past's honeyed voice, and alluring words, as well as my blatant disregard for the Future when I tilt entirely away from it.

The rare moment when I switch between left and right is when the Present catches my attention and my heart skips a beat, like it does when you first figure out you're being watched. Those obsidian eyes seem to be constantly peering right into the very core of my being, in spaces I wouldn't even know existed if I hadn't followed his gaze. The Present knows everything that happens at the table. He seems to understand the mystery of Future and the charm of Past, despite the fact that he is never really looking at either. For I am the sole recipient of his fixation, which is not as flattering as it sounds.

I hold on to the notion that I can somehow convince myself that he's nothing but a phantom. A non-being, an empty seat, just a figment of my imagination. But I can hear his breathing loud and clear, punctuating each moment and keeping a tab of my life. It makes me want to hold my breath and hope against hope that this is just a dream. That if I stop breathing for a minute, I'll wake up gasping but wake up nonetheless and be free. But he's still here, sitting across from me with the air of an interrogator – intimidatingly quiet. Which means he knows it all, that he can't be fooled or manipulated. This only fuels the constant fear I have of one day hearing his voice when he finally does speak. A sound that'll shatter all illusions, like a breeze blowing away the haze before the dawn breaks. The defences that you hold, the pretences that you keep, the reassuring hypothesis and the hopeful optimism, all of it sublimating into a wispy nothing. Can you imagine that?

I am terrified that the moment he asks a question will be the moment I fail. It will stun the Past into a fading silence and force the Future further into the shadows. Only two left at the table, under the blinding light of the truth. The Present, still unbothered, will lean back and fold his arms over his chest while I struggle to catch my breath. He will keep watching and this time I won't be able to look away. Losing myself once again in a different kind of gravitational pull, one that untethers and propels, one that jerks you awake, sobering your delusions and turning you to face a self no longer marred by the sheen and scars of yesterday, nor confounded by the blindfolds of tomorrow.

That will be the day I look up at the Present without fear, without the anxiety of all that I know and all that I'm afraid to know. I will see him for what he is, a gift bestowed upon me by the universe itself. The chandelier will gentle its light over us as we sit together, no longer bothered by the shadows or the silence, comfortable in a discourse of our own. And, in his knowing eyes, I'll be able to see that the time that has gone and the one yet to come, is not mine. They can no longer hold my reality. The only thing that truly belongs to me is the moment I'm in and the life therein.

Fragility of Being Human

Siddhanth Pai

Embarked on a journey
To find where my soul belonged
The antique store beckoned to me
Archaic and celestial
The doors cradled realms within
A connoisseur's paradise
Alluring remnants of history

Deafening booms roared off the veil of dust
Akin to ash over Pompeii
The antiques spoke an alien tongue
Whispering fables
Of lives once lived
And stories once told

A porcelain vase had me fixated
Delicate, floral etchings
Bore semblance to a vast meadow
Figure hourglass like one of Michelangelo's muses
Cradled it in my arms while I placed myself
Gingerly on the chair

Humans are fragile too
My mind juxtaposed
Cracks and scars adorn my body
Tears cascade through a chasm in my eye
Fragility is inherent, for a child cries involuntarily
When a mother lets it go

My eyes, unleashed rivers, at the sight of someone
Placing white lilies on a loved one's grave
The vase I held was broken
For rugged surfaces conceal the frailty within
Human life is a dance in discord too
For our resilient form shelters a delicate soul

Aren't we dainty flowers in the garden of life
Waiting to be plucked one by one?

Sweet

Djuna Hallsworth

"Does it look streaky?" I follow Natasha's gaze down to her exposed legs, which are tinted a shade that some marketing department has dubbed "African Savannah". I was with her when she bought the fake tan from Priceline on the promise that it would deliver a look that was "bronzed and exotic".

"How can a tan be exotic?" I had asked her at the time, squinting at the product with unconcealed scepticism. Natasha had shrugged.

"Dunno. How can a wax be Brazilian?" she countered. I had to concede I didn't know.

There's nothing exotic about the way she looks now, though, at 4:40 on Friday afternoon, unless you interpret *exotic* as a euphemism for *odd*. I fiddle with the chunky bangle she has lent me, wondering if I'm overdoing it with accessories, if we'll look like we're trying too hard: her with her garish skin, me with my garish jewellery.

"So?" Natasha prompts me again, palms pressed onto her hip bones. She does that when she feels defiant and insecure at the same time, like she has to compensate for the latter by manifesting the former. "Does it?"

I feel my nose twitch involuntarily. She always says she values my honesty.

"I mean, yeah, obviously."

My eyes travel back up to her face and I shrug apologetically.

"It's just really bad, right?"

I focus my gaze just above Natasha's head, wincing at the prospect of confrontation. It's rare but it does happen when you touch a sore spot for her. She looks furious for a moment, then catches sight of herself in her full-length wardrobe door mirror. Her reflection peeks out between full-page lift-out posters of Rihanna and Justin Timberlake and cut-out inspirational quotes from teen magazines that impressionable girls are certain to find and internalise. *Flaunt it. Just be-u. Confidence is sexy.* Compared to the airbrushed limbs of the pop stars, Natasha's legs look almost diseased.

Realising that nothing we say can fix the mess, Natasha's furrowed brow gives way to the half-moon eyes and curved lips that accompany her bubbly laugh. "Oh my god. You're right. It's so *gross!*"

"Yep," I confirm, now laughing too, partly with relief and partly because it's kind of funny how companies can make such wildly inaccurate claims about the performance of their products and never be held accountable. "Can you wash it off?"

"Noooo," she laments, studying the especially irregular patterns under her knees. "It's meant to be gradual, not instant. Though it is instantly rank."

She turns this way and that, examining her carrot-tinted body from various angles, as if one of them might miraculously offer a more flattering perspective. I take a swig of my watermelon-flavoured Bacardi Breezer and consider our options.

"Leggings?"

"In the wash. I wore them in Phys Ed yesterday."

"Ew, why?" It's only April, not cold enough to justify the extra layer under our baggy sports uniform.

"Because I hadn't shaved my legs and Mrs Pierce told us she would be off getting a skin-tag removed." Natasha turns to look at me with an *isn't-it-obvious* look.

"I don't get it." I invert the bottle and suck out the rest of the sugary drink, then replace it on Natasha's dressing table next to an unopened one. We have an allocation of two alcopops each while we're getting ready: that's all her sister Talia would buy us. Natasha asked as sweetly as she could if we might borrow a few splashes of flavoured Absolut Vodka from Talia's extensive and enviable collection which she proudly displays on a bookshelf in her bedroom, but apparently Talia had just snorted and rolled her eyes. I crack the lid of my second Breezer and sip the now room-temperature drink. It tastes like a teenager pretending to be sophisticated.

"Well, have you ever had a sports substitute teacher that wasn't a hot guy on his prac?" Natasha asks me in her best morning show presenter voice. I consider this.

"No."

She taps her left temple with a gold nail paint-tipped index finger. "And they call you the smart one. He was actually only average, I wouldn't really have cared if he saw my hairy legs, to be honest." She turns back to her reflection and mutters, as much to herself as to me, "What am I going to do, though?"

Her shoulders slump forward in resignation and for a weird moment I feel a surge of affection for the girl I've spent the most time with, by choice, out of anyone in my life. It's stupid and unimportant, but it's also major deal: our first real party, our first chance to shake off the school kid persona, even if it's just for one night.

But my head is swimming a bit from the alcoholic sugar rush and thoughts seem to dissolve before I can put them into words. We deliberately didn't eat because Talia told us the drinks will hit harder this way, and because we need our stomachs to look flat if we're going to impress anyone, though I'm more dizzy than tipsy. I squint, as if tightening my features will somehow tighten my perception.

Somewhere in the distance, channelled through cheap speakers, Fergie is breathily spelling out the word that we're dying for people to use to describe us; a word that evokes oversized white sunglasses, fake fur-cuffed cropped jackets and curling iron curls, not the plastic bra straps, boob tubes and tousled two-toned layer cuts thick with styling mousse a la the suburban quotidian. Glamorous. We are destined for better things. G-L-A-M . . .

"It'll be fine. We'll fix it. You'll look hot." Maybe it's the song, maybe it's the four percent white rum in the fizzy drink I'm downing way too quickly, but I seal the promise with an uncharacteristic wink.

Natasha straightens up, rolling her shoulders back and catching my eye in the mirror. "Yeah, duh."

* * *

The bus driver raises his eyebrows at us but says nothing. The bus is not full, but delinquent kids are sprawled out, leaning across the aisle and over the back of the seats, taking up as much space as they can. I guess they have to compensate for feeling disempowered in basically every other setting. There's one spare seat next to an older woman who stares fixedly out of the window, and another next to a Chinese man with several large plastic bags of groceries in his lap. I nod to Natasha to take the seat next to the woman. Some kid behind me is playing a 50 Cent song on his phone, but it sounds more like interference than music coming out of his shitty Motorola E895. I have the same phone but, if anybody asks, I'm about to upgrade it.

Natasha takes out the aerosol can of instant tan that we picked up from the chemist on the way to the bus stop and bends down to spray the front side of her legs. She's changed into pinstriped short-shorts and a figure-hugging vest over a push-up bra, with stilettos that I'm sure will snap any moment, just like the pencils that Jordan Moffatt snaps during science whenever the teacher asks him to stop spitting rhymes while she's teaching. No one knows how he's ended up with such a steady collection of pencils, but our educated guess is that he steals them from the lottery kiosks at the Galleria.

The tan smells like fake coconut and chemicals. It doesn't take long before the woman next to Natasha registers the potent synthetic smell. She sniffs the air, then looks at my friend with undisguised disgust.

"Do you have to do that here?" she demands to know.

Natasha widens her eyes at me then turns to the woman with feigned remorse. She thinks she has a knack for talking to adults, but I think it's more that they can't be bothered to challenge her bizarre logic.

"I'm so sorry but I do, actually. It's Melissa Varga's party tonight and we don't want to look like dorks." The woman tuts and reverts to staring at the deserted footpaths that rush past. The bus takes a sharp corner causing Natasha to lurch towards the aisle, spraying tan across the floor. I'm sure the driver is speeding, but I don't blame him: shuttling misfits from one unfortunate suburb to another on a Friday night can't be much fun. When we alight, I make sure to call out "Thanks!" but not before shooting a dirty look at the kid with the Motorola.

* * *

We don't know Melissa Varga, but Natasha works with someone who does. It's her eighteenth and everyone knows that you need the biggest possible turnout at your eighteenth, even if you don't personally know half the guest list. When Dani Fairlight leaned across her checkout at work and said to Natasha, "Hey, you wanna come to Melissa Varga's eighteenth on Friday?" Natasha didn't say, "Who's Melissa Varga?" She said, "Okay. Can I bring a friend?"

"Prob'ly," Dani had replied. "I'll text you the address. Dress code is 'look hot but don't be a skank.'"

We take abrupt steps in the dark – teetering to stay upright in shoes we've only ever worn at home where the floors are carpet, not concrete – and wonder how we'll recognise the birthday girl.

As we approach the suburban community centre that Melissa Varga has hired out, we realise we needn't have worried. We can see her through the wide glass windows of the flat-roofed brick building, surrounded by clones of her in singlets and bubble skirts. She's wearing a white birthday girl sash and has a helium balloon with eighteen on it tied to her wrist. On a trestle table behind her is a pile of wrapped presents; somehow, even from this distance, although concealed by wrapping paper, I can tell they're expensive.

"Shit, did we get her anything?" I ask, even though I know the answer.

Natasha shrugs. "It's fine, we probably won't even talk to her."

A single, bulky bouncer standing at the entrance says he wants to see our text message from Dani but hardly bothers to look when Natasha shows him her phone screen.

"Don't get pissed. I have friends in the cops," he mutters as he holds the door open for us.

"U+UR Hand" is blasting out of two speakers set up in either corner of the space, which has been adorned with more helium balloons and various pink tissue paper decorations that I'm sure I've seen at the Reject Shop. No one would admit it, but we all shop there, regardless of what kind of cars our parents drive.

"Let's get a drink," Natasha says, grabbing my arm and pulling me towards a self-service bar.

"I dunno, that guy is friends with the police," I remind her. She scoffs.

"Yeah, and he's getting paid fifty bucks an hour to not call them. Basically everyone here is underage, anyway."

Bottles of Brown Brothers moscato are wedged into silver bowls of ice, next to which are neatly aligned rows of stout plastic wine cups. On the next table are bowls of crisps, Coles antipasto platters and tiered cardboard stands of pink cupcakes that my mum bought for my nan's eighty-sixth last November. I take the moscato that Natasha hands to me and head towards the food.

"Don't," Natasha insists. "You'll bloat."

"True." The dizziness has passed and now I'm just thirsty. Not for wine, for water, but I don't want to ruin our pre-drinking by effectively hydrating myself.

I sip the sickly moscato and scan the sizeable crowd, unsure if I'm hoping to see someone I know or hoping not to. If Dani

Fairlight is here, Natasha either hasn't seen her or doesn't care. We hang back; after all, we're here to be seen, not to socialise. I look good in my blue minidress and strappy wedges, and I'm stoked to finally have the chance to try out the smoky-eye look I learnt from *Dolly*, which I've only ever trialled at home and then washed off before mum could see.

The problem is not how I look tonight, though, it's how I look every day at school, in my moss green polo shirt and black nylon skirt, with hair that I've neither bothered to straighten nor curl, and makeup that's too heavy to be barely-there but too light to make me pretty like the-prettiest-girls-in-our-year Annika Burke and Carla Waite. We have each other, me and Natasha, and between us we have a fair few friends and no notable frenemies. That should be enough. I get better-than-average marks and I come home to parents who are interested in how my day was. It's more than enough, I know.

The Sugababes sing about feeling confident in how they look. *Easy for you,* I think. *You're not sixteen.* The song is changed before it gets to the chorus: not the right vibe. Now East Coast rappers are extolling the traits of a "nasty girl".

"Hey."

I know I don't want to be a nasty girl, but I also know it's not up to me. It's never been up to us.

"Hey?"

"Oh, hi." A guy has approached me. I hadn't noticed any guys and wonder where he came from, then notice a group of about eight of them on the far side of the presents table. They were probably concealed by the mountain of metallic wrapping paper and gift bags.

"What's up?" He swigs from a bottle of Hahn 3.5. He looks familiar; I think he's in the year above us.

"Not much." A posse of Melissa Varga's girlfriends squeals as a new arrival shuffles her way towards them in her chunky platforms, yanking down her animal-print minidress so she doesn't flash everyone.

"What's your name?" the guy asks.

I contemplate giving a fake name in case I do happen to see him at school, but decide this would make things more, not less, weird.

"Amy." I raise my cup of moscato.

"Zach." He taps his Hahn 3.5 against it. "Cheers." He's not bad looking: kind of messy, dark brown hair frames an almost-symmetrical and mostly acne-free face. I confirm that he is from our school; I recall him from school assemblies and sports days. Not a champion, but competitive nonetheless. He clearly doesn't remember me, but why would he?

"So, how old are you?" he asks.

"Why?" I retort defensively. At the same time, Natasha leans across me. I'd almost forgotten she was there. "Eighteen," she purrs.

Zach laughs. "Yeah, nah. There's no way you're older than me."

Natasha raises her eyebrows and shrugs in a way that suggests she's indifferent to whether or not he believes her. "Maybe we are."

She's a flirt. She gets attention and she likes attention. I don't know which came first but it hardly matters at this point. I get it: it's her thing. We all need a thing, or else there's nothing to put in the yearbook. Just, sometimes, I wish she wouldn't, so that I'd have some space to have a thing, too.

"We're sixteen," I concede. I hear Natasha click her tongue maybe because I told the truth, but maybe because he's talking to me and not her.

"Sweet. What school do you go to?"

I suck a breath in. I long for a time when the question is not a conversation starter and the answer won't matter.

"Uhh, same as you, actually." Maybe honesty is my thing.

"Oh, right." Zach looks puzzled. "Sorry, I guess don't really pay attention . . ."

"To the younger kids? I get it."

He nods. "Anyway, maybe I'll keep an eye out for you at lunch!"

An image floats into my head of Zach approaching me in my daggy uniform, the skirt a size too big because somehow my post-puberty hips might "grow into it", my shoes heavy on my small feet, my oversized backpack lacking any trendy branding, my legs slowly reddening, not tanning, under the unforgiving midday sun, my whole self an uncomfortable, ill-fitting version of the other girls in my year.

"Oh god," I mumble.

"Huh?"

It's what inside that counts and all that . . . but I feel better on the inside when I look good on the outside. Don't we all?

But I summon my best sultry smile, anyway, because you have to start somewhere. "I said, 'sounds good.'"

This House Has Too Many Rooms

Chloe Isabelle Pryce

within these walls I keep a room
for every woman
who ever thought herself beloved
for each girl whose only wrongs
were place and time

come, my sister –
lay your head against my chest
I'm sorry they will have to miss you now:
your children, friends, your kin
I'm sorry that you counted him among them

his rage – possessive, vile –
should not
have tolled your final hour
it should have been adoring,
that last touch you ever felt
against your skin

come, and I'll uncrack the splintered ribs
unsplit your lip and douse the flames
his betrayal was the oldest, cruellest crime

I see it all –
your amaranthine sorrows; salt-spray joy
your swift, wine-bruised resolve
I see the love you gave him, how you raised him
I see the way you started
for the door

forgive me –
I cannot lay your absent bones in softer ground
I cannot grant you sun, or one more season
I cannot make men kind

but come, my sister,
to the house that I have built you
and in these endless halls I'll keep you warm

*For Khouloud, for Isla, for Mavis, for Evette, and for all
our sisters*

In the Depths of Winter

Vanessa Yenson

The WhatsApp message begins with #DeathNotice – no forewarning or soft lead-in.

BAM! Next time, why don't you reach through my phone and shake me awake?

A heaviness drops in my chest as I read through the details. I linger over the fact that it's not an unfamiliar feeling these days – like a pebble breaking the waters of my consciousness, creating ripples of discomfort. He's the third man to die in the past four months and I am not sure how to grieve anymore. I stare at the June frost outside my window – three rosellas perch in the wattle tree, their red and blue feathers stark against the sodden greenery.

The first death was Mum's brother-in-law, Peter, who left for his daily run in the Manchester countryside on a cool morning in February and never returned home. I remember him as a gentle man with a wicked sense of humour. He was wiry and fit, ate healthily and enjoyed the odd tipple. He loved his wife and family, and he loved his work – a sixty-three-year career that began in the Royal Air Force, continued as a test pilot and then, in his final years, he rewrote the flight crew operating manuals for a commercial airline. His life was rich with numbers and planes, sons and granddaughters.

The last time I saw Uncle Peter in person, was at a spit roast lunch at my cousin Chris's house in Kent nine years ago, a reunion for Mum and her four remaining sisters. The tantalising smell of the slow-turning meat nips at the edges of my memory like the wasps that darted about that day – flying everywhere – into the kitchen, around the garden and directly at us. Chris, his niece and I were recreating a photo from fifteen years before. In my favourite action shot, a wasp is a blurry missile in the foreground, heading straight for the phone while we laugh in the background, amused that I am now the shortest in the group. Later in the afternoon, Uncle Peter rallied us in for a group photo and we all squinted into the sunshine and smiled. Since that day, the five sisters have not reunited in person.

"All I remember is Peter whipping you around the dancefloor," my Aunty Val says almost every time I see her. It is a memory from her son's wedding in Toronto, when I was still using a walking stick after cancer treatment and all its insidious side effects. "I was just worried he'd fling you too hard and you'd go flying."

The second death in May was Dad's brother-in-law, Ignatius. The previous year, Uncle Ignatius went kicking and protesting into a nursing home in Vancouver. It wasn't the same nursing home that his wife Frances went to when her dementia deteriorated – where they could peer at her through the window during COVID but were unable to speak to her, to console her. There needs to be a word to describe the lost connection during that time, when people withdrew into themselves, forgetting the comfort of love through physical touch. I am grateful that their daughter, Candy, received government permission to dash from Sydney during lockdown so she could sit with her mother during those last days.

The last time I saw Uncle Ignatius in person was in Hong Kong fourteen years ago, when we made a pilgrimage to our ancestral village in Southern China. He was quiet but always had a ready smile and a twinkle in his eye. Uncle Ignatius and Aunty Frances had owned a corner store in Johannesburg, South Africa. They had emigrated to Canada after being held up at gunpoint, saved only because the firing mechanism jammed. I can imagine them both remaining calm in the moment, perhaps not fully exhaling until they landed in Vancouver.

"Eat!" Aunty Frances had said at yum cha, piling more dumplings and meat in front of me. I shook my head politely, but my protests were futile. When I pulled my bowl away, she deposited more food onto my saucer. Uncle Ignatius just smiled, slowly helping himself to more *har gow*. The conversations in Cantonese buzzed around our table – washing over and around us in unseen currents and eddies. Aunty Frances shook her head and clicked her tongue with disapproval when I stammered that I couldn't possibly fit any more food in. Uncle Ignatius patted his belly and winked at me.

The third death, the one announced in the WhatsApp message this morning, was Rodney, my mother's old boyfriend from the 1960s. I learnt about him after I came across a sepia-toned Polaroid of a smartly dressed Chinese man leaning back, gazing into the distance. There was an inscription to my mother, signed "All my love, Rodney." It was an awkward feeling – thinking of my parents as young and single, imagining the love they had for previous suitors before they committed to each other, the hearts they broke or the people who had broken theirs. The concept of courtship via letters and dates to the movies, wearing sixties flares with Brylcreem and beehives, makes me smile – as if I can peek through a portal to the past, where life seems simple.

The only time I met Rodney was in the nineties when he visited Australia from South Africa with his wife and children. It was a hot, sunny Christmas when the only relief for us kids was diving into the pool. After lunch, the aunties settled around the mahjong tables; the clatter of the tiles and the chatter of the gamblers mingle with the afternoon heat. The men huddled around the hexagonal dining table, red Bicycle playing cards flicking out a new game, while fingers shuffled piles of poker chips, contemplating their odds.

I looked at Rodney's two children, trying to imagine myself with them, as them. After the party, I hugged Mum and Dad. Had Mum walked a different path, I would not exist and she might still be living in Johannesburg.

* * *

Intellectually, I know there was so much life lived in the years between these select moments and when they breathed their last. In my mind, these three men are trapped in time – forever younger and happy, before the restrictions and depression of Covid and before my own recent brush with mortality.

In September, during a family video call for his wife's birthday, I saw Uncle Peter in a little Zoom square on my laptop. I had joined the late-night call with my parents and aunties and uncles from Australia, England and Canada; two even joined from their futon mats while holidaying in Japan. I will be forever grateful to the technology that united us – stretching out to the edges of the world where family had dispersed and settled, drawing us together – enabling us to laugh, reminisce and share stories, even if we talked over one another when the internet connection lagged. There was news to tell and milestones to celebrate – this togetherness filled my heart and made the conversations feel timeless and precious.

In December, Candy shared a video of her father in the nursing home. Ninety-six-year-old Uncle Ignatius was dancing to *Que Sera, Sera,* hand-in-hand with a female staff member, who was dutifully wearing a mask. There were Christmas lights in the background and other residents watching on. His steps were small, and they both faltered as her Santa's hat snagged on his arm when he tried to twirl her. There was animation and joy in his movements, and he finished with his arms raised and a giant smile on his face.

In April, after suffering monthly chest infections, I relented and called an ambulance. It was close to midnight – my blood pressure and oxygen saturation were perilously low and my temperature was high. I couldn't keep anything down, but I just wanted to stay in my own bed and drift off to sleep. Hospitals, with their needles and x-rays, central lines and drips, were a nightmare from my past that I was keen not to revisit. Time stretches and warps within those encroaching walls; days and nights blur into weeks; consciousness mingles with dreams, memories and pain. You forget the sensation of the sun on your skin and the brisk autumn air against your cheek. You become less than – a slave to mealtimes, visiting times, change-over times and ward rounds. You surrender to the routine as if you are nothing more than a cog in something much larger than yourself.

In May, Rodney's son Greg posted photos of his dad's eightieth birthday on Facebook. Greg and I had not been in touch for years, so it was a surprise to see this milestone pop up in my newsfeed. I marvelled at how well their family looked; it had been thirty years since they visited Sydney. I smiled at their pride for Rodney. Greg had wished his father many more years of good health. It's sobering to realise that this morning's WhatsApp message has come less than a month after his birthday celebration.

Death, in all its forms, seems to be circling me these days – tapping me on the shoulder, silently screaming at me to wake up and hold each moment just a little bit longer – to articulate the feelings I have before they pass and hug a little fiercer. As I watch my parents age, I acknowledge that we are all getting older, keenly aware that nothing lasts forever. And yet, they shove any notions of "getting old" back in my face when I serve to them in our weekly tennis matches and they sprint to angle a cross-court forehand winner. I can tell they've been practising during the week – their competitiveness keeps them sharp.

I think of Chris and Candy and Greg – all navigating unfamiliar paths without their fathers. Different shades of grief – those whose fathers were wrenched from their lives suddenly, unexpectedly and those who shuffled towards fate, wondering if their next farewell would be their last. I wonder how my family felt when they stood around my hospital bed in April, tube down my throat, machines breathing for me.

As for me, I think I am still processing the news of these deaths, grasping the concept of an empty seat at the dinner table. There's a numbness – as if I have just emerged from a heated pool in the depths of winter, when the icy contrast takes your breath away. I know my limbs are there, my brain acknowledges the proprioception of my body in space, but I do not trust myself because I cannot feel. There's a disconnect due to the time and distance, and I wait for the delayed sorrow to hit.

The memories of these men, of my parents and of happier times give me strength as I recover, reminding me that I am part of something bigger; the emptiness and shock are consequences of love and togetherness. And I am reminded that even after the harshest of winters, life will find a way to heal.

Attraction

Toby A. Moffatt

My breath is a universe of stars – motes of frozen white in the dark of this narrow corridor before they fade away. I cannot deny that cryosleep is an exceptionally convenient way to traverse galaxies, but my footfalls tremble with the ache in my knees and I flex my still-chilled fingers as I walk away from the arrival bay. There is a chill trapped in my lungs as I emerge into the expansive welcome terminal.

The steel grey shine of the floor and walls is disrupted by market-tested deep blues. Carpet strips, faux-plush seating. The wall facing me from across the vast hall is one single pane of glass overlooking the breadth of space. A canvas of black not just speckled with dots of stark light; gentle brushstrokes of fading embers and slumbering violets, flecks of glowing gold and silent midnight blues. As I approach, the view of space grows. The trappings of the welcome terminal fade away in the periphery. The darkness at the centre grows. Not an errant inky spill but a break in the canvas – fixed and present. It is the black hole we named Messier 88, drawing in the universe in a silent, steady breath.

I place my hand against the pane between us as though I might push through and past the frayed edges of the canvas into you, Messier.

To slip into your depths.

Something glides in front of you – silver, around the size of a shoe box. There is no way of knowing what it contains, but I imagine a punnet of saplings inside, green growths peeking just above the surface of the soil. Perhaps the gravity would draw the plants tall and thin or instead quash them altogether. Perhaps the time dilation would return burgeoning stalks ripe with fruit or instead we would be withered on our own vines by the time they returned, unchanged. I imagine that the scientists that work here at the Messier 88 Observation Deck, meandering at the edges of your continual inhalation, already know the outcome of my speculative experiment – but I cannot conceive what the effects will be on more complex organisms.

My now warm breath fogs the glass.

I draw back my hand, pulling the sleeve of my jacket over the fingers and wiping away the condensation to reveal you once more.

A voice comes from behind me.

"Ah. There you are."

I turn to face the speaker, whose long lab coat is wrapped around their wizened form.

"I hope I didn't keep you waiting too long. Come, let's get you settled into your new quarters and then later we can begin your orientation to MOD – the Messier 88 Observation Deck." They turn and begin to leave.

I follow behind them, fingers still and footsteps sure as I turn to let my gaze linger on you before departing.

* * *

Every day since my arrival, I have sat at the same table flush against the glass wall of the cafeteria with two chairs on either side and facing one another. Today is no different. I set down my tray – plate of spaghetti in a smooth red sauce, banana, pulverised green fruit smoothie – and sit, resting the curve of my jaw in my propped up hand as I gaze out to you.

My lips brush the skin of my palm as I murmur.

"Hello."

The darkness between the lights and colours of space are tresses, long and winding – the hair of your figure slumbering among the stars, knees drawn to your chest and clutched by your arms. Stirring from dream, the shifting of your dark head and dark locks is measured in obfuscation. Light blinking in. Light blinking out.

"I thought . . . we might share a meal. I think you may like this – that it may even be your favourite."

Those tresses are a writhing mess of fine, inky pasta. Twisting, squirming strands being inhaled into your abyssal mouth stained with sauce. The cosmos unravels and unwinds, drawn to your lips in a meal for you to consume.

"How are you?"

I recently overheard one of the scientists discussing a historical technique for the representation of data called sonification – where visual data is translated into sound, into song. Perhaps your voice would be low and mournful. Perhaps your song would be long, drawn-out notes on lines pulled tense and rising. Perhaps your words could sparkle and shimmer in constellation with mine.

"What was that?"

"Huh?" Spaghetti spooled in my fork hovers just above the plate and I look away from the window – over to the person standing beside me who spoke.

"I thought you said something. Were you speaking to me?"

"Ah . . ." I set down my fork and turn to face them, hands folding in my lap. My eyes fall to the floor for a moment before looking up to the person – lab coat and grey hair. "No. I wasn't."

"Oh."

My eyes begin to drift back towards the glass and out to you. My body follows.

Their voice does too.

". . . Sorry."

My brow furrows. A silent pause before footsteps recede.

My hand once again provides a pillow for the side of my face, elbow propped up on the table. Shifting, my back hunches – as though I might shield our conversation from the rest of the cafeteria. A nebula of gentle pink settles on my cheeks.

"Sorry about that." My gaze slips away from you for a moment but then returns as a smile plays on my lips.

That stretch of darkness from you to the spaces between the stars is a smile.

"Where were we?"

* * *

Despite all our lunches together, my appetite for you remains unsatiated – so I set out to my nearest resource allocation kiosk to change that.

The one nearest to my living quarters is a pane of blue-tinged glass set into the steel wall – long and wide enough to show me the upper half of the person staffing it and the ends of several shelves behind them, stretching away. Set into the glass is a small black circle with a thin green line, and beneath the glass of the kiosk are an assortment of dark, rectangular outlines of varying sizes that can fold outwards, enabling the transference of items.

"Hello."

The green line pops on the first syllable and wobbles on the second.

"Hello. What can I help you with today?"

"Ah . . . I was wondering if I could borrow a tablet. For half an hour."

"If there is something wrong with your tablet then we can organise a temporary replacement while we fix it. I'll just need the tablet and for you to fill out –"

"No, no. My tablet is fine. I just need to borrow another one. Just for half-an-hour."

Just so no one can review my searches and wonder.

There is a crease in the forehead of the person staffing the kiosk, a deep, vertical groove between their eyebrows.

"Why?"

"I need to look up some stuff."

"Stuff?"

"Stuff."

". . . No one is going to know if you use your own tablet to look up porn."

The green line crackles with the jagged edges of my inhale.

"Forget it."

"No, wait." Their brow is still furrowed, but a mischievous light dances in their eyes. "Be back in half an hour or I'm reporting you stole a tablet to look at porn."

I glimpse a flash of their grin before they turn away to stroll down the shelves behind them. Pausing, they select a tablet and come back. One of the small openings below the kiosk glass opens, tablet inside.

"Happy watching."

Scowling, I return to my room. I immediately draw the dark blue curtains over my porthole windows – hiding you from view – then switch on my desk lamp. Taking a seat, my thumbs hesitate over the screen. My eyes flick to the covered window, holding for a second before looking back to the screen. My fingers dance over the surface.

Your data log is revealing.

Your history. Your properties. The way you contrast and compare to other bodies of your size, of your type.

And your photographs are intimate.

Standard photography could not capture you but direct radio images of your core reveal what is beyond my own sight; your arms drawn around yourself and your body aglow, like the embers of a fire smouldering in the shared intimacy with those who draw near.

No green line betrays the absence of my breath.

My thumb hovers just above the screen, just above that image of you laid out before me. Could I bring myself to touch you, to cross that barrier as I scroll down the page?

My thumb caresses your edge before sliding along the glass.

* * *

"It's hard to make out, isn't it?" The tourist's voice dribbles from their lips, barely seeming to struggle in rising from their throat. They curve their hand over their opposite wrist, smoothing over the sleek shine of a form-fitted spacesuit.

"Pardon?" Turning, I face them – and a politely practised upturn of my lips follows.

"It." They draw their hand away from their wrist and feebly flick it out towards the depths of space – out to where you lie. "Messier."

"Messier 88." Meeting their eye, I earn myself a simple scoff. My attention returns to the glass and I walk over to it, placing the tips of my right hand's fingers against it. ". . . They are kind of . . ." Nails brush along the surface until my finger pads start to stroke along the glass, stroke along the edges of your form. ". . . Here," I murmur.

"I don't see it."

"Well –" I snatch back my hand, clutching it clenched against my chest and snapping my gaze back to the tourist. My eyes narrow, straining as I push the corners of my lips into the facsimile of smile. "You will. You are very lucky, you know. It is a rare treat to be allowed to be close to them. Messier 88."

"I'm not sure luck has much to do with it so much as a tremendous amount of money," they sigh, regarding the apparently far more interesting sight of the bed of their nails, fingers curled in over the palm. "Suppose we'll see."

". . . Suppose you will." I wave to the door behind them with a flourish. "If you step through, the team can begin the next stage of preparation for your spacewalk."

"Oh, very well."

They leave.

My body trembles.

". . . It's not fair." My voice is breath. My head whips back in your direction, both the lights of space and the darkness of you reflecting in the tears swelling along my eyes. This may be as close as I ever come to holding you. "It's not," I sniff, driving the heels of my palms over my eyes and shaking my head, clearing them and looking back to you.

Silently, you float there – ever the attentive listener, whether over lunch in the cafeteria hall, or in the snatched moment as I walk between the chambers of the observation deck, or through the small porthole window of my living quarters as I start to drift to sleep. On the winds of your breath drawing in the universe, I feel the excessive beats of my heart and urgency of my blood slip away, a ragged breath escaping me.

"You're right, as always." I smile.

"We'll be together soon."

* * *

The inside of the airlock is a featureless, white cube where even the edges and corners blur away. I know that I am facing the wall that will open to the outside because it is directly opposite the wall to enter the airlock, which is directly behind me. There are no seams or lines inside here to suggest these walls will open, but they will both part if bidden.

When the airlock opens to space, I imagine it will be obscured by the fog of my warm breath on the inside of my space helmet. It is impossible to distinguish now, but excitement embraces my body and squeezes my heart – drawing out wheezes of laughter that echo back over my face, dancing over my ears.

I lift the data pad in my hand, holding it at the periphery of my sight to see past the expected plumes of my own breath painting the glass of the helmet. There is a light, hatching texture built into my spacesuit where it clings over my fingers, enabling me to tap in an eight-digit numerical code.

Confirmation: Final safety checks on the equipment of all airlock occupants have been conducted?

Rolling my shoulders, I jostle the pack strapped to my back that funnels oxygen into my suit and enables propulsion through space.

Yes.

Confirmation: Final checks on the tethers for all airlock occupants have been conducted?

The ports built into the wall from where thick cables are drawn remain unopened, the white of the airlock remaining uninterrupted. The belt around my waist serves only to help secure my pack to my back.

Yes.

Final Confirmation: Open airlock doors?

Yes.

Air blasts over my body in a snap of movement as a seam splits the wall in front of me from floor to ceiling. It then bolts open, the data pad flying from my hand as I am sent rocketing into space in the grasp of a hand unseen.

Yours, of course.

The universe of stars – both the literal beyond and the metaphorical as near-infinite pinpricks of condensation line the inside of my visor – washes my world white and I hold my breath. I hold my breath and it fades away, darkness creeping in at the edges and slowly revealing you until I can see you at the centre of the universe – the centre of my universe. The lack of light does not reflect my smiling face back at me, instead projecting it on and into you – a tether by which I am connected and drawn to you.

Reaching down, I grasp the handles of my pack and compress my thumbs into the buttons there. The backs of my legs warm with the rockets that are engaged, and I lean my body forward in your direction.

Don't (You) Question

Ngoc Thuan Anh Huynh

i never wrote a poem without rhyme,
and it's only recently that i realised,
despite having crafted words since childhood,
as if something is coded in my blood.
even in art, i need principles and rules,
unable to break free into the world's endless creativity pool.
my lyrics flow, like water, shaped by the corners they touch,
but never fly, like dandelions, soaring through stardust.

"it's the norm, it's tradition,
it's the easiest way to separate wise ones from peasants."

"study all from the textbook,
even if your heart is twisted, turning you crook."

("cherish your treasure: comb your charcoal hair,
gowns covering knees, no skin bare.")

"stray from the guidelines, you will be punished,
losing the good girl badge with every new idea you pitch."

("stinky are the ones who dare ask,
question the society and everything it masks.")

those same words keep ringing in my ears,
fuelling my pens with fear,
and whenever my tears blur the rhymes out of shape,
the whispers of the past curl slowly by my nape.
so the moment i try to pour my heart out in art,
all my courage falls apart.

Belonging (To Be Longing)

Ngoc Thuan Anh Huynh

Dalgo devoted himself to a new story, something birthed from the ambitions of retelling Mary Shelley's *Frankenstein*, a seed planted by the innate ache to materialise and immortalise all the word-shaped fogs that had been plaguing his mind. The prologue blurred his nights and days together as Dalgo bathed in his own visions, a scenario no different from any other writing session of his.

Not until he reached *the part* – the climax, the question that the entire novel centred around, the six words that hooked all his other thoughts into darkness – did Dalgo stop. His neck craned to the side to see daylight tiptoeing from the window to his desk, his body letting the beats beneath his chest and the subtle movement of his diaphragm ground him to reality.

What was so precious about life?

He frowned, rearranging the words in his head:

What differs between life and death?

Staring at the photo of a man next to the laptop screen, his smile blinding, his hair swept to one side, Dalgo found himself drifting to his memories, floating somewhere between June and July, where summer sparkled, drawing constellation after constellation on droplets of sweat scattered across his and the other's skins. The heat's overwhelming being eased the sizzling of their hands brushing, calling all of Dalgo's senses awake.

Maybe *that* was the answer.

People were born to be whining babies with no ability to make life-changing decisions. People were born to be the reincarnation of Aphrodite, now named Peter, or the ordinary exhausted writer who hopelessly yearned for him. People were born to have the happiest day of their life falling between June and July, with flowers blooming in their chests at the sight of *someone's* beam. People were born to ponder their own existence. People were born to face mortality salience in every waking moment. People were born to know they have limited time on Earth, so they had better say fuck it and crash their lips to the man to whom desire consumed their whole soul, despite the looming knowledge that the other just revealed he was rejecting mortality.

People were born to stay humane. People were born to die. People were born to beg the love of their life to *not go*.

* * *

Dalgo's heart was palpitating in desperation, so loud yet so weak, the way every human's body tweaked and used all of its remaining energy to seek another second of survival. Icy silence wrapped around his vocal cords, freezing any words in his throat, locking all the "nos" and "pleases" along with his tears.

Dal wanted to scream. To kneel and beg. To burn this whole laboratory surrounding them down. To do anything to prevent Peter from signing the contract. To freeze time. Twisted in his stomach was less of an anger and more of a hurricane, urging his legs to stand between the doctors and Peter, hands shaking the latter awake from his immortal fantasies.

Maybe he did freeze time, considering how he couldn't even lift a finger right then. He could only stand at the entrance, features settling on blankness, brown eyes devoid of mist, watching the love of his life going through another physical examination before the entire operation proceeded as if he was an audience of some live TV recording. The room's brightness hurt his head. The words in his larynx fell apart into vowels and consonants, then letters and strokes, until they didn't make sense anymore. Though from deep down inside, he knew no logic existed in the first place, and even if it did, it'd be merely a scratch on the strong walls Peter's stubborn ass always had to shield his opinions.

Because the love of his life chose Project Resurrection.

Because he was here as an emotional support, not as an option to the younger man.

* * *

"What do you think about it?" Peter asked, voice laced with excited giggles. He was lying on the couch – specifically, Dal's lap – basking in the relaxing feeling of the older man's fingers dancing through his soft hair and massaging his scalp. The yellowish light that Peter had hung in their living room hugged his face, tracing from his sparkling eyes to the mole under his plump lips, from his sharp collarbone, peeking from the loose pyjama top he was wearing, to his raised left hand, now made of metals and plastics.

Dal closed his eyes, his breath becoming shallower with every beat of time passing. It had been a week, yet he couldn't bring himself to look at Peter's synthetic hand, especially when it was only the beginning of Project Resurrection and of the rest of the other one's life.

It was all written on paper. Starting with the hands, over the next few decades, participants of the project would gradually replace every part of their bodies, until the point when they no longer needed to worry about their physical state deteriorating or their flesh and bones wrinkling with old age. In other words, they would be immortal.

The knowledge of what that entailed was a horror story to Dal, despite Peter's chuckles when he revealed his true thoughts about the matter. Someone would live *forever*, would be fearless of the concept of time, would see death as nothing more important than dust, would wear youth on themselves in a permanent, vampire-ish way, would have to witness everything they know change and everyone they know leave Earth. They would get to know new people only to bid farewell to them again. They would hold others in their hearts only for the loved ones to realise in solitude that they would eventually get left behind in the "past." He irrationally started to fear for Peter. The human's hands had two jobs – to grasp and to let go. Dal didn't ask about what Peter's synthetic hand could do, whether it was able to shoot lasers and all of that, but he couldn't help but wonder, *will my love, with his big soul and his bigger heart, manage to let go of what he once grasped?*

Humans are dreamers. Thanks to their dreams, they wrote, they invented, they created. No plane or book blossomed without the seeds of an idea planting in someone's head. Being a novelist, Dal should have known this more than anyone else. He crafted his dreams into pages and chapters, squeezing cries and laughs out of thousands of individuals all around the globe, navigating them through nineteenth-century mansions with genderqueer scholars using their entire beings to suppress his overwhelming longing for another man and the present time's everyday setting with dark morals and darker desires, but not the future. Never. Whenever Dal tried out the science fiction genre, immediately and automatically his cowardice limited his mind to neon lights and flying cars, to androids and another plague, and nothing more. The uncertainty of the future scared him to no end.

Dal wasn't like Peter, who didn't let any boundary pin him down, so brave, wild and free that Dal used to joke he really was a Peter he knew from his childhood, the boy who knocked on windows with his shadow and a glowing fairy at midnight and refused to grow up. To grow *old*.

What made Dal feel so much for Peter became his biggest nightmare, tearing him apart every time he laid in his bed and thought about how the younger man dreamed so big that Dal and his stupidly ordinary, quiet life, with his boring morning schedule (bathroom, butter noodles for breakfast, train, office) and devastatingly long routine before bed (Korean drama, skincare, meditation, occasional vanilla sex), could never satisfy him, that he had to keep running away and reach out to some scientists to expand his lifespan, to find more time to fulfil the dreams he never could make come true with Dal.

Dal's hands were still intact, so he could grasp Peter's synthetic hand and let him go.

"It needs to grow on me," answered Dalgo. "I need *time*, I guess."

* * *

The human skins were uniquely beautiful. With his eyes blindfolded, Dal could misjudge linens as cottons or wrongfully label glasses as plastics. Yet, with just a mere touch, in a split second, he could tell if it was Peter's cheeks or belly under the tips of his fingers.

Peter's scars were ingrained in Dalgo's memory the way they were on the younger man's skin. On his hips, there were marks from a fight with Peter's brother when they were in elementary school, and there was another one on his right ankle, shaped like a crescent, a result of falling down the stairs in his paternal grandparents' house. Dal mapped every scar with his lips over the years, till the point he knew Peter's body better than his own. Any sensitive button to press. Any dip to dive.

And one day, Dal's smile faded along with the scars. Peter's new parts were flawless, smooth and *real*, but they radiated no heat. There was no imperfection that Peter used to shyly try to hide from him, only giving up when Dalgo insisted on caressing and whispering to his skin loving words, voice dripping honey, stating he would love every inch of the younger man if Peter ever allowed him to.

Desperately, Dal tried to kiss the other's body until he could bring the warmth back. Seconds stretched on, with the absence of all the love and pleasures those intimate moments usually gave them. Though the younger man remained quiet, Dal could see from his blank stares that he was devoid of feelings too. The hollow void inside Dalgo expanded and expanded, until it almost swallowed his entire existence.

He laid his cheek on Peter's bare stomach, finding assurance in the way his diaphragm moved up and down next to his forehead, where fine lines and dark spots were starting to form clearly.

* * *

Dalgo was not a big philosophy fan, but these days, he kept finding himself thinking about the Ship of Theseus paradox: would an object still be the same object after having had all of its original components replaced?

Would Peter still be Peter, when all of the parts his mother gave him were removed?

Dalgo never told the other man about this thought. In fact, long gone were the days of Peter lying in Dalgo's lap in their living rooms, chatting about anything and everything.

Silence was a greedy monster. It filled the space between them and just kept growing, until the voice of the love of his life got swept from Dalgo's memory.

Without him, the world outside his window still moved, even with a crazier pace, pulling Peter along the current, while occasionally letting him come home to check in on the things that he was so ready to leave behind: the weathering plants they had, the promises they had shared forever ago and Dalgo.

Vocal cords weakened from disuse, the older man said nothing about the blankness that gradually became a default feature on Peter's (still devastatingly beautiful) face, willing to veil his eyes with delusions. His fingers twitched to comb through the other's hair, long and dyed blond, with a silly need to see what was going through Peter's mind. He didn't, yet somehow, as if he travelled back decades ago, when their souls were even more intertwined than their physical states, he felt something deep inside that left bitterness on his tongue.

Humans were dreamers.

And Peter had stopped dreaming.

Belonging

Angela Fossi

I never wanted to be here.
Does that sound morbid?
My home might be on another planet,
or maybe in another realm,
flying my feathered wings to my angelic home,
anywhere but here, please.

Still, I searched, but never found my tribe –
the steady beat of my heart called to my abode.
Sometimes, only angels and fairies
welcomed me into their world;
I found them in books and paintings,
the only places I belonged.

But as I walked a deeper spiritual path,
my shadow grew bigger than the sun;
the shadows of others reflected me,
through loss and heartache.
I grew through tears to reflect my light.
Despair, a ghost that often perseveres,
but now, I feel a sense of belonging

to mother earth. My connection
to other humans still hard to find,
but a friend I found in a feline –
home is the care I give,
and her purrs are a hymn in my lap.

Just one small person reflected in billions
of other beings, all part of the one –
our tribe may be found in the familiar,
our tribe may be found in the unfamiliar.
If we can greet one another
with an open heart and an open mind,
meeting somewhere in between,
the differences we find in each other
can be a gift waiting to be received.
Our tribe may be found in the familiar,
our tribe may be found in the unfamiliar,
but the light of our souls is one and the same.

Now You See Them

Karen-Anne Coleman

Mrs Davies put a photo of a Tasmanian tiger on the classroom wall. It's above my desk. It stares down its long nose at me all day. It's standing on concrete with a wall behind it. It looks scared, like the photographer's flash is a headlight and it's about to be skittled. Or maybe it just misses the bush.

Bec sits next to me. She and her family went to the Northern Territory last year. They weren't supposed to come back. They went for her dad's work. But then there was an accident and they were suddenly back. Bec's brother, Dylan, didn't come back though. He's buried up there. In the red earth. Everyone says how dry the soil is up north. I wonder if the earth where Dylan is has dried up so much it's cracked. I want to ask Bec, but Mum said not to ask Bec questions about being up north.

Mrs Davies says the Tasmanian tiger died out and isn't coming back. People thought they were annoying, made mistakes and didn't keep them safe. She says there are lots of other animals we could still lose.

Actually, what I should have told Mum when she said not to ask Bec questions is that it doesn't matter because Bec doesn't talk. Not anymore. Not since she came back. Last year she liked playing fairy gardens in the corner of the playground, in the bushes where it's shady and hidden. But Helen says we're too old for fairy gardens now anyway. She says we have to play makeovers. I miss fairy gardens, maybe Bec does too.

Bec and I like drawing. You don't need to talk to draw. We draw animals with big eyes and cute faces, huge heads on tiny bodies. We colour them in and I give them names. We've got a big collection. They've got their own little families and go to school and work and the doctor and have babies. It's a whole little town. Penguins, seals, sloths, otters, foxes, whales, red pandas, white tigers, elephants, polar bears, hippos . . . all our favourites. Bec is a really good drawer. I'm not so good at drawing, I write little stories for the animals. I've glued some of the stories into this notebook. I don't want anyone else to read this notebook though.

Last year Bec's mum used to pick her up from school. Now her dad does it. He's really tall and smells of tobacco. Mum said he was an environmentalist. The way she said it made me think he wasn't anymore. Or maybe he wasn't him anymore. I dunno why Bec's mum doesn't come to into school anymore. Maybe she had to get a job if Bec's dad isn't an environmentalist anymore. Or maybe she's just tired.

Mum never picks me up from school. I walk myself home. Or sometimes I walk with Helen, if she doesn't have anyone else to walk with. Helen has five brothers. When we walk by her house you can tell if they're home 'cause there's lots of noise, people shouting and thumping and jumping. My house is always quiet. Sometimes Mum is out when I get home, sometimes she's asleep in her room.

Helen's place has the steepest driveway I've ever seen. The house sits like a fort at the top. In the mornings, when it's cold and frost tips out of our mouths, Helen's dad screeches the car down the driveway, swerving at the last moment to avoid the thick tree trunks on the other side of the road. Helen's dad is an Important Man. Everyone says so. Helen's mum fell in love with him when she was doing important things too, but she doesn't do important things anymore, she just stays home while Helen's dad goes on being an Important Man. Still, even though I know he's an Important Man, every time I see his red, blinking eyes over the steering wheel I'm convinced this will be the day he's crushed in the gully at the bottom of his driveway.

If there's too much shouting at Helen's house she keeps walking to mine. She likes putting on my dress-ups. Mum has given me lots of her old clothes. I even have some of her old lipsticks. They hardly have any of the smooth, bright colour left, but it's enough for Helen. She smudges "forbidden fuschia" and "vamptastic plum" onto her thin, dull lips and blows herself a kiss in the mirror. I don't like how the lipstick makes me feel like a suffocating stick insect, so I leave her to it. Instead I run the black lace of a slip through my fingers, letting it trace spiderweb shadows across my hands.

Helen says not to tell other kids at school that she comes to my house. I'm not sure why. I wonder if Bec would like to come sometime, but I don't want Helen to be there when she does.

* * *

Mrs Davies says we are going on an excursion soon. To a museum in town. We'll catch the ferry. She gave us worksheets with pictures of all the different animals that will be on display in the museum. I don't understand why the animals are in a museum instead of a zoo. There's an enormous insect the size of a lobster. When I think about how its fur rises off its twiggy, long legs my skin goes goose-pimply. There's the sweetest little wallaby, it looks like a brown bunny. When Mrs Davies

141

explained how one of the wallaby skulls was found up north she looked up at Bec and stopped mid-sentence. She told us all to turn to the next page. There was a tiny Tasmanian tiger pup floating in a jar with its paws curled up, skin wrinkled and ears floppy. Its eyes were closed so softly, like it was waiting patiently in its mummy's tummy for its turn to be born. But the jar never opened. Something dripped onto my page. I looked up at the poster of the Tasmanian tiger above me. I thought a fat tear had dropped down its long nose onto the paper. Then I realised it wasn't the tiger's tear, it was Bec's. She sniffed and wiped her nose on her sleeve. Then she started drawing, with her face low to the desk, so I couldn't see. When the lesson was over she gave me a new bunny-wallaby for our collection. I smiled and called it Hairy. I think she liked that – she smiled back. But she screwed something else up in her hand and threw it over the desk into the bin. At recess, after she left, I scooped it out. It looked kind of like a stripey wolf. Its eyes were more scared than our other animal drawings, but it was still cute. I knew Bec didn't like it though so I put it back. It must be tricky getting things to be exactly how you want them.

I'm not really sure how to ask Bec if she would like to come to my house. I've never asked Helen. She just comes. I don't think it's up to me.

Sometimes when Bec's dad comes to pick her up, her mum is in the backseat of the car waiting for them. She winds down the window and stares at the school gate, but I don't think she really sees any of the people going in or out. I try to smile at her as I walk past, but I've never caught her eye. Once I saw Bec get in and there were crutches lying across the middle seat. I don't remember the last time I saw an adult in the back seat of a car. I walked home with Helen that day and was happy when her house was quiet enough that she went in, because I really wanted to be alone so I could untangle my brain. I made myself a peanut butter sandwich and lay on the brown grass in the backyard with my legs in the air until it was nearly dark and Mum came home.

The next morning I did something I've never done before. Instead of walking past Helen's house on the way to school, I ducked into the gully next to her street. At exactly the usual time, I heard her dad skidding out of a collision and knew Helen would be waiting for me. My shoes were sinking into the soggy mud and my skull muscles twitched, but I stayed quiet. I swatted a mozzie on my arm and saw the bubble of my own blood burst out of its overfull belly. A frog was croaking over and over nearby. I was sure he'd give me away. I waited and crouched until my legs prickled and ached. When I was finally convinced Helen would have left without me, I squelched through the creek, feeling my socks sponge up the murky water. I was worried about leeches but had no idea how to spot one or what to do if I found one. When I finally clambered out of the little patch of sunken rainforest and onto the bitumen outside the school gate, the bell was already ringing. I sprinted into class and, panting, slopped into the chair beside Bec. Creek mud dribbled from my shoes. I didn't look at Helen. She hasn't come to my house since then.

The weekends at home can be a bit boring, especially if Mum needs to sleep in. I try to find things to entertain myself. I have an imaginary friend who lives in the mirror. She's easy to talk to. She has the funniest expressions and ways of using her hands when she talks. She loves to dance. Mum always gets mad at me for putting handprints on the mirror when I've been chatting to her. She thinks I'm talking to myself and calls me vain. Mum needs the mirror so she can see what she looks like each evening. I wish Mum didn't have to go out. I've told her

I want her to stay home and bake cookies and read stories and hug me all night. On good nights we bake the cookies, sing and dance, and eat the cookies still warm straight off the oven tray. She invents stories better than any fairy tale and waits until I'm asleep. On bad nights she says she needs the extra cash, puts on the TV, kisses me and tells me not to stay up too late. On those nights I usually fall asleep on the couch.

Sometimes Mum and I look after things for people. There's a lady who drops off dogs who are waiting for their new owners. The dogs stay with us for a little while until someone else comes to pick them up. I like most of them. Sometimes they're a bit rough and then we have to put them in the yard and they howl, which makes us all sad. One time Mum came home with a really stinky old man who had no shoes and slept on our couch. Mum said she often walked past him at work and he had nowhere else to go that night. When he left she scrubbed the couch. I've never seen her scrub the couch before or after. Of all the things that Mum and I look after, my favourite are the kittens. They get dropped off in a cardboard box and tumble over each other to explore or cuddle or fall asleep in my lap. Even when Mum goes out it's nice to have a kitten asleep in your lap.

I asked Mum what she does when she goes out. She said she tells stories mostly. I'd love to be able to tell stories the way Mum can. I wish my stories were as good as Bec's drawings. Bec doesn't complain but maybe if she starts talking again she'll expect more from a friend.

* * *

I asked Bec if she wanted to come to my house. She didn't actually nod or shake her head, but she looked at me sideways, like she was a scientist and I was a strange creature she had found in the forest and needed to classify. She drew a graceful black and yellow striped frog for our collection that day. I know you think a frog can't be graceful but this one was. It had eyelashes. Not the kind of eyelashes you paint onto your face, the kind that dance. So I took that as a good sign.

I decided Bec probably didn't know if she could come to my house, so one of us had to ask her dad. It wasn't like with Helen. Helen could just wander off whenever she liked. Bec's mum and dad always knew where she was. So I had to be bold.

When the bell went that afternoon I bolted out the door. I had to get to Bec's dad before he could bundle her up and away, and swaddle her into their home where I couldn't reach her. Bec's dad was pulling the car up to the gate, her mum was sitting in the backseat again. I stopped mid-stride when I saw her. Her eyes were scared and sad, exactly like the Tasmanian tiger above my desk. I wondered if she had ever seen the picture of the baby Tasmanian tiger in the jar, and how she would feel about it. But I shook my head, remembered my mission, and took off again towards the car. I was sprinting around to the driver's door, to target Bec's dad, but stopped as another car squealed around the corner. Helen's dad narrowly missed the pavement as he drove away. He was early. Helen stalked out the gate, her wide nostrils daring anyone who looked at her to ask about it. No one did. By the time I had stopped blinking, Bec was in the car and waving to me as they drove away. Her mum gave a little wave too. There might have even been a smile.

I've never been very good at telling stories. I get all muddled and forget where I'm up to. One of the kittens Mum and I had once was a beautiful grey tabby. She had blue eyes like a cloudless sky. Mum said you could see through to the horizon in them. Her chest and paws were a milky white. We'd put out a saucer of milk and laugh as it dribbled down her chin, wondering if that's how her fur had got that way, staining herself with milk. She'd fill her belly like a fat water balloon and roll over, exhausted with the effort of keeping it all in. As she got bigger she wanted to explore, Mum said to keep her inside but she kept clawing at the back door. She was only a few months old when she went underneath the screeching tyre. Her insides were so red. Smeared across the road outside our house. The lady who brings the kittens said not to worry, these things happen, but not to let the kittens outside.

When Bec drew a soft grey kitten I tried to tell her about our grey kitten. I didn't tell the story as well as Mum would have. But I tried.

Bec's mouth creaked open, like a rusted hinge, and she said, "You don't always see them." Then she paused, looked down at her hands as she finished the drawing, and added, "My mum says I can come to your house." I smiled.

The Same Blade

Simone Wong

is it ownership? someone asks me, peeling the
goose-bumped skin of the orange to reveal the
supple flesh. is it *that* kind of belonging?
between us: a scuffed oak table, two lattes,
three languages, a half-peeled orange,
and the gaping unfamiliarity of firsts.
they repeat, is it ownership?

i tell them, no, the earth was soft when she gave birth to me
and the seraphic blue of the sky sounded like a major chord.
music dripped onto her belly, my belly, and it
was a sweet thing, being attached and limb-like.
i imagine tears on my cheeks, mine and hers,
like a baptism – the awakening of our shared skin.
nowadays i forget when i started to call my face "ours".
between us: a mirror refracting light, only light.

someone offers me a peeled orange, but it is too sour.
she used to cut my fruit into wedges every night
and somehow her slices were cleaner than mine
though we wielded the same blade.

inheritance is a strange thing, not something you own
because it can't be turned over or bartered.
i think of a river, the current tumbling over
sticks and rocky fragments and notches of scraggly roots,
outpouring invariably to the sea.

it's not me to her, not her to me – it is beyond our two
insignificant bodies of water.
we belong to the ocean, she told me once,
and i understood.

Woodwork

Dennis Haskell

Neat slivers of timber curl into the air
as my father slides the plane across
and across. Whatever he is making
is already shaped in his mind, in a way
I can't imagine. Six decades ago:
all his tools are hand tools, all
his labour has a human dimension.

He stops, quickly writes measurements
on offcuts, walls, whatever
with his flat carpenter's pencil,
his hands quick, steady, sure.

High school, first year we had woodwork:
I planed a pointless hunk of wood
until it went from horizon to arc;
the teacher awarded a pass,
as bare as my chippie skills
and I never had that class again.
Self-consciousness saw my carpentry off
and I was sent to study Latin instead.

Although he never said a word,
somehow, I thought my father proud
that I escaped labouring for necessities,
the province of the urban poor.
Now, sixteen years older
than my father ever was,
a small part of me still believes
that writing, talking and deskwork
aren't really work at all.
I love timber of any kind,
upright lecterns, the symmetry of cupboards,
the grain of teak, the lightness of balsa.

Even now a whiff of sawdust
in the nostrils has my father
at his handmade workbench,
a piece of timber in the vice's mouth,
his left hand firm on the black front knob
and his right on the plane's back
with a perfect scything rhythm
shaving hours, years off the sombre air,
Caesar hacking his way through Gaul,
and me, not much taller than the bench
holding the sandpaper ready, so like him
in so many ways, so close, so far.

Mangiare O Non Mangiare

Alessio Maugeri

A long table surrounded by dozens of friends and family both distant and close, yet all under the same roof of love. From the kitchen come four men with flour and dough staining their bodies, carrying out a wooden board. There's a rainbow of unlimited selections of food atop the board. The beautiful brown-black slices of bread, cooked to perfection by fireside, rest in the centre of the board, the map to guide through the oceans of flavour ahead.

Westward are meats, a spectrum of pinks and reds sliced fresh from the back of the kitchen. Mortadella sliced so thin that it practically wraps around the tongue, with small bits of green olive in each slice adding a kick to each bite. Prosciutto drizzled in a thin coat of oil and salt, complementing the tenderness of the woodfired bread perfectly. Salami sliced in thick parts directly from the sausage, tough on the jaw in a satisfying way. Further west comes calamari, with brown-yellow batter, a fluffy yet crunchy texture that soaks in dashes of lemon juice perfectly.

Eastward of the bread, lies all sorts of vegetables and cheeses. Deep black kalamata and smooth green Sicilian olives bask in a salty, spicy brine together; a small ceramic tray next to them to hold their seeds. Further east, a large clump of burrata leaks onto the rocket and prosciutto base beneath it.

At the board's end, roasted mushrooms, and charred peppers and artichokes, dark in colour and richer in flavour.

Though the attendants have plates, none bother themselves with them. Hands stretch across the table eagerly for whatever catches the eye first. Prosciutto and mortadella are thrown haphazardly into the mouths of the hungriest men, the more delicate and careful ones wrapping it around the bread and eating it as a complete meal. Juices of the burrata slowly trickle their way down and off the antipasto board, the unlucky people sitting in front of it in charge of wiping it up when it drips onto the table. An uncle's son is trying to spit his olives pits into the small tray from where he's sitting, but keeps missing and has them fall into the lap of the cousin across from him who's fighting the urge to throw them back at him. All the *nonnos* and *nonnas* at the end of the table are conversing loudly about the old days or the loyalty of their children. Their grown children, who sit towards the centre, hear their harsh criticisms, but dutifully take bread and salami to their parents and young children. In the background, some classic Italian musician's most beloved music plays, but the noise of the feast completely drowns it out.

Everyone at the table is everywhere, and to be everywhere is to be with everyone. Noise is community, food is compassion, and to share is to offer the soul. Seated at the table, you are loved deeply, and you love everyone deeply. In taking the first bite, the taste of home floods your senses.

Nothing Rhymes with Orange

Yenfay Camp

How often do we find ourselves here,
Skin prickling, bare again barring our clothes:
Paper into air, ravenous flames birthing green smoke,
Alight, agleam, weightless as opaque whisps twist into the
    glistening black above;
Light, now hollow, shot back onto itself –
Time ever moving, infinite yet held,
A thousand millennia tucked into a cloudless wink.

In slow breath I watch you watch me:
      A world split in two, green landmasses balancing
      atop a swirling glacial sea,
      Dilating pupils pooling at silky moonlight,
      refracted in the quiet still of summer's bite,
Only departing periodically behind heavy lids,
your hide-and-seek to my sherried smile.
      I wonder, can you hear
      the constellated whispers in my eyes?

Do you ever trace the overlapping flecks, some stars others
    scars,
As they unfurl back in time, a flower past its prime,

Once full like a yawning tulip waking on the eve of all,
Now weary and heavy and drooping as the afternoon falls?

Young, I learnt *nothing rhymes with orange.*
Back when girlhood shone bright like fresh snow:
     Pink satin in the autumn breeze,
     conjuring woodland elves with ease,
     Dandelions twirling like fairies mid-flight,
     Carrying my hopes with them
     across the softening blue sky.

Mum, hair thick and glossy, upturned in a knot: a black so
    deep no light dares cross it.
     She's calling me in, down the stairs,
     my feet again on polished oak,
     Dinner steaming at the table:
     Yao-Fan. Oily rice. *Your favourite, my little heart.*
Dad, opposite me, blue eyes kind, hair white and caught bright
    in the kitchen light.
     After, always a round of nashi-pear:
     crisp and sweet, two hands holding one slice.
     After, always a round of story time:
     the secret adventures of Teddy as he sat,
        Matted from love,
     Beside me, bowtie of black ribbon,
     Always so polite, so stagnant,
        When watched –
        Dad the author, Mum the revered critic.
     In the fading glow of dusk, whenever I would smile,
     they would too.

Older, still young.
She stares back at me, through me, into me:
into my veins, my blood, my marrow.
Into the blues beating phantoms through my heart:
I am, I am – still, I am.
She looks like neither of them, neither does she resemble the
    others:
        Blonde, blue-eyed, creamy and laughing silver bells.
        Beautiful in the correct way, the others.
        Made for the screen, the others.
        She eats weird food, say the others.
        Is almost, but not quite.

        I blink.   She blinks.
        Left arm raised.   So is hers.
I open wide, bare my teeth, snarl.
Wide, blistering white, snarl.

        Switch flicked – finally, she leaves, but as do I.

An amalgamation, two halves of safe and ordinary.
        An intersection, one whole of unknown,
        extra ordinary.
                You're beautiful as snowflakes are beautiful.
                Uniquely beautiful.
                Unique, by virtue, is   alone.
                nothing rhymes with   orange.

So alone, I took to spinning daggers,
my words my sword and shield.

Talons out and checking pulses, burying promises, cold, in the
field.
My tightrope, wound tight through time, remained sharp,
without an inch of slack.
Spinning in circles, feet raw and bloodied, always did I flay the
peel:
Every hello a mirrorball,
every goodbye some vitriolic gall:
Pick your poison, I said to them,
for poison is poison is poison is me.

Reserved to collecting collapsing stars, I sat and watched the
scorched earth scream:
Every anointment a masculine silhouette,
Every night, sleeping, a loaded gun under our bed.
Yet still I'd run, back against time, tripping over my best-laid
snares,
My arrow drawn, shadowy wood,
empty black save unanswered prayers.
Until all these lines became erased, at once I assumed both
predator and prey,
The ink bleeding crimson until all that remained:
Nothing rhymes with orange.

And so I vowed to keeping afloat, never to dive again,
And I didn't – you did, catching me on the way down.
Yet when I landed, expecting ash, I found only bright orange
unfolding from my back:
No more talons, no more spears,
just marmalade, dazzling, instead of fear.

Calm, you listened, calm, you heard.
So tenderly did you unshackle me;
Gently, you lifted this cross from my back, kissing away my
   myopic attacks.
Rhythmic were your footsteps, as into the fire my alienation
   you threw,
And beneath our feet, out of dead earth, Eden again sprung
   and grew:
      Tangerines and sunsets and the overflow of Autumn,
      Apricots for breakfast, the sun on the horizon.

So as we lie here, yet again, your curls dark in my lap,
Feeling the air rise and warm as dawn shines through the
   cracks,
I exhale and meet your eyes through the smoke,
      For whenever I smile, you do too.
And at once, within reach, the lights of home flicker alive
   around me: *Nothing rhymes with orange*, but you and I
   don't rhyme.
We're more the same atom halved; what salt is to sea.
      Orange, meet Orange: a belonging that reverberates
   through my being,
      As bliss is to tranquility.

Uncles

Dennis Haskell

I wake early, but still three hours behind
much of Australia, and waiting patiently
on the phone's ever alert screen
is a text from a cousin I hardly see:
his father – my uncle – this morning died.
Half-foggy with sleep, I'm not sure what it means;
I can read the words all right, about
my mother's youngest brother – last of the tribe,
the last of my aunts and uncles
to disappear from the earth.
Later, my cousin will tell me that it means
we're now the cavalry, riding towards them.

* * *

Uncles: when I was very young, they were
all around me. Five families crowded into
my grandmother's small, rented house:
the working class in the 1950s. How
we all slept there, I'll never know,
I was just a wide-eyed, watchful kid.

My mother had brothers before and after;
my oldest uncle, Ken, was a cheerful bachelor.
In my teens he taught me to drive;
on weekends I kangaroo clutched from
pub to pub, from TAB to TAB,
throughout Sydney's stretching, wayward
Western suburbs. I mostly stayed in the car
while he went in and did his dough.

Uncle Ron, short-ish, chest shaped
like the kegs he lived for,
boasted that when doctors
swore him off the drink
he would "line his stomach"
with milk, then hit the grog.
What deep-set, sunken bravado
makes a man live mainly for beer?
He always seemed carefree, cheerful,
straightforward, and died young.

             Uncle Keith was the youngest:
while we kids searched for sixpences
in the pudding we hated to taste
he would pull out thrillingly
clean five-pound notes, and
point to his unfailing luck.
Outside Christmas, he always sought
struggling shillings and pence.
His boys young, my brother and I
sat in his tiny, windowless van

handing paddle pops across the seat
while he drove ringing the ice cream bell;
in time it felt like a dungeon on wheels.

Or else we sat on the back
of a table top truck, no seat belts
but hills of bananas and oranges
to hold us in. Paper-bagged, we
walked them from door to door –
mothers were more likely to buy
from imploring urchins;
at day's end we sat on the truck
outside the pub, sipping lemon squash
amidst the leftovers, waiting for uncles inside;
the stench of all day-ripened bananas
inhabits my nostrils still.

* * *

My uncles lay down with no dreams intact.
For all the talk of post-war boom,
this was the Sydney of tractable battlers,
their Sydney not the city of the fingering
glistening harbour or the golden sand,
wave scuffing beaches
but of suburbs where trams and buses
and rattling trains clattered them to work,
tacky in water and tenacious heat
with their jokey comrade, Manuel Labour.

A Sydney of milk money left outside,
of unlocked doors and corner shops,
food grown in gardens and goods on tick,
of a time and a blood we all shared.

Seven Mile Beach

Tom Evans

Our faces were cast down, shrouded by our hoods and bitter cold as we walked slowly across the puddles of water along the coastline. Each step was a gamble between sharp shells on soft heels or murky water between our numb toes.

"Watch your tips," Grandpa would say, as the thin fibreglass points of our fishing rods dropped precariously low, pulled taut by the barbed red hook fastened on the golden spools of blue reels.

It was too early in the morning for anyone to be around. The roar of the waves against the rocks was replaced by a gentle lapping of smooth porcelain water that kissed their jagged surfaces. The wind was only a whimper.

On our final approach to the start of the beach, lichen covered the last outcrop of rocks before our feet could find the refuge of soft sand. We couldn't help but quicken our pace as our aching arches finally found the damp familiarity of Little Beach's sand.

Two brothers were either side of me, one holding a tacklebox, the other a fishing net. Behind us, Grandpa was slowly finishing his journey across the rocks to the start of Seven Mile Beach. For a moment, we stood in silence, staring in wonder at this old man unphased by the barnacles and oysters underfoot as he looked up at us at each step, a wry smile on his face. The soft breeze carried the wisps of his white hair off his weather-beaten face, which was punctuated by his strong nose pointing towards us.

It was the smell from the rusty bucket swinging by his side that we would always remember from those early mornings. Its contents, the defrosting remains of bait and burley from previous outings, were our secret weapon for the morning ahead.

Now was the time to look not below us but outward, to the outgoing swell across the horizon. As we walked along the beach, we would peer at the formation of the waves that came rolling in – searching for a break in sets that signalled a sand gutter, a small refuge for fish in the sand that protected them from predators.

The stretch of sand was vast, stretching all seven miles as it wrapped around the deep blue expanse of water that went as far as our tired eyes could see. We walked closer to the water, the biting cold against our toes and feet waking us up with the forced immersion.

"Here should do it," Grandpa said, as he adjusted the collar of his quarter-zip jacket. He lifted his skinny arm and directed his open palm shakily at the sandbank ahead of us.

My oldest brother carefully laid out an old beach towel, stained and bloodied but most importantly dry, then he put his fishing rod on top so that grains of sand wouldn't get into the lubricated parts of his new fishing reel. My brother and I followed suit before Grandpa handed us his rod and began submerging his bucket of burley in the water.

Then, Grandpa removed a net of fish guts from his bucket and waved the net along the sand in time with the water. As the sea retreated, hundreds of small holes emerged in front of him in a brief instant.

These tiny holes that one would assume as indentations made by shells or debris on the beach, on closer inspection, were actually the writhing heads of hundreds of beach worms. The intoxicating smell of rancid fish was too much for them to resist. Their heads writhed in the wind, hundreds of tiny legs pulsating on either side, desperate for a taste of rotting flesh.

Grandpa worked with a deft touch to catch a worm, waiting patiently for another wave to crash against his ankles before waving the fishing net in a large arc in front of him. This time, he pinched the head of a bait fish from between his thumb and forefinger and waited for a curious victim to pop its head out close to him.

In a flash, he crouched over the worms closest to him, lowering the bait just above the wet sand. We huddled closer to watch, but not too close as to scare away the beach worm, which raised its head slightly higher than the others. It could smell the food was close and as Grandpa lowered the bait ever so slightly, it latched on to flesh.

A game of patience, Grandpa couldn't move too much, or the worm would shoot back down into the sand before he had a chance to react. He was aware of the next set of waves that were approaching, and the timidness of a worm that would retreat at even the smallest feeling of wind.

But Grandpa knew exactly what he was doing. His back shielded the southerly wind and as the next wave was seconds away, his right hand slowly reached behind the worm and bait, thumb and forefinger encompassing the arched back of the creature.

Once his fingers were around its slimy body, its muscles tightened and it attempted to shoot back down in the sand, but it was all in vain. Grandpa waited for the worm to slightly loosen its strain before pulling it straight up from the sand below.

What looked like a small head had become an impressively long and thin beach worm writhing in Grandpa's hand as he triumphantly looked towards us. He chuckled to himself as we half-heartedly congratulated him before we realised that it was our turn to catch our own bait if we wanted to fish.

One at a time, we took slimy pieces of fish from Grandpa's bucket and found our places on the wet sand. Without the expertise of a wise old man, we each grasped onto rubber pliers to assist the delicate process of uprooting worms from their home.

I found my place closest to Grandpa, wanting to show him that I could do this on my own, yet uncertain of how my fingers, stiff and without feeling in the bitter cold, would be up to the challenge. In a much less graceful action, I threw the net of bait out in front of me as the water receded. There weren't hundreds of heads that popped out of the sand like before, but there are enough for me to lower the piece of the pilchard in my hand over unsuspecting prey.

With great caution, I readied my pliers as the worm slowly arched over the bait in my hand. But, as soon as I moved to get in position, it shot back down, leaving me empty-handed. I sighed and looked towards Grandpa who could only offer a grin – his interest was rapidly waning as he knew the rising sun meant he was running out of time to get bait on the hook.

That was Grandpa though, his calming presence was one of subtle encouragement. A nod, a smile, sometimes a pat on the back. It was never over the top or too muted, but just enough for us three boys to feel welcome, to feel safe.

When I think about moments like fishing on Seven Mile Beach, these are the times where I really felt like I belonged.

Moments where the shouting and tears of home would melt away with the salty sea spray and defrosting fish guts to a simple act of joy. The joy of adventure. Even though these fishing trips and other adventures slowly waned as we reached high school, then university and beyond, those mornings waking up at the crack of dawn in the freezing cold, catching slimy beach worms with fish guts and coming home empty handed were some of the best memories we'll ever have.

"I got one!" My older brother would shout against the breaking waves, hoisting a worm nearly as long as himself into the air for Grandpa to nod and smile. It would take several attempts myself, but soon my little brother and I also had a collection of worms in Grandpa's bucket, ready to wet our lines and begin what we came here so eagerly to do.

The long beach rods that we had carefully laid on the towels were now lifted high above. Quick adjustments were made to the ringlets to make sure they all aligned perfectly and that the braided line was not fraying or knotted. We tied a simple paternoster rig to a thick leader the night before, a heavy star weight hanging from the end of each rig. Like always, we were expecting a big haul of fish. And as always, we were most likely to be disappointed.

Still writhing in the bucket, the worms had to be cut to size and threaded through the barbed red hooks so that they covered the surface but still dangled their ends over the hook. With surgeon-like precision, the worm had to be pushed through a razor-sharp point without pricking ourselves or tearing the bait off.

Once each rig was set and baited, we walked in unison directly out towards the water. Grandpa made it up to his ankles, my older brother his shins, but my younger brother and I made a point to venture out to our waists, the water lapping against our oversized board shorts and the bottoms of our faded shirts.

Scanning the horizon, Grandpa flicked his spool back and rested his index finger against the line on the base of his rod. Next, he pivoted on his back foot and swung the rod behind him, perpendicular to the sand. After a brief pause, in one effortless motion he transferred all his weight and momentum onto his front foot, pivoting on his front foot as he whipped the rod over his head and let go of the line at the perfect time. The hooks and sinker flew through the air in a perfect arc, landing in the middle of the break in the waves.

Try as we might, my brothers and I could not reach the bar of sand where the fish were undoubtedly hiding, despite being so far out that we were up to our waists in water. But the moment was not wasted being here, together in the freezing cold with the sun only just rising on the horizon.

But here we were, just as we had been so many times before during the school holidays. Shouting words of encouragement to each other, waving to Grandpa as he stood still with his finger feeling for any sudden change in the slack of the fishing line. Sometimes the best moments were when we said nothing at all, just standing there side by side, gazing out into the vast expanse of the ocean – anticipating, waiting.

At any moment this sense of peace could be replaced by the whirring of the line from a reel and the familiar words of "Got one!" as we gathered around the lucky recipient of a fish caught on the line. The collective thrill of a rod bending as a fish fought on the other end – with no knowledge of what type, how big it was, or if you were going to land it – was a moment made all the more sweeter with family who had been there for the ups and downs of broken lines and the snags on seaweed.

This time it was me struggling to hold on to the beach rod when my reel began to whir. In fact, the line was leaving its spool so quickly that it created a screaming noise. I struggled to loosen the tension in time as the line rapidly depleted, showing no signs of slowing down.

"Wait, just wait," Grandpa would say in a tone that pierced through the rampant mutterings of my brothers and I as we stood wide-eyed trying to guess how massive the fish was on the hook.

In a rhythmic motion I began to pull the rod up, then reel in as the rod was lowered and the line went slack – repeating this action ad nauseum, just as I had learnt from Dad all those years ago.

This was a true battle with a fish, unlike previous fishing outings with Grandpa, where the goal was to catch small sand whiting for him to make a mouth-watering pasta with pipis. No, this time the rod bent further and the reel screeched louder than ever before.

Each pull and reeling in became harder and harder. The line began to be pulled with such ferocity that I struggled to keep my footing on the sand, with my Grandpa and brothers close behind to steady me if needed.

"Don't give up," Grandpa said, grabbing my shoulder and squeezing as my wrists began to ache. In that moment it wasn't like battling a big fish off our boat, but something more primal. With two feet planted firmly on the sand, toes sliding below the surface with each step moving forward and backwards, the swell picked up and the wind's gentle breeze began to build with rapture.

As exhaustion began to set in, even with such support around me, I felt alone. With Dad gone and Mum unrecognisable from her previous self, it was these trips to the beach with Grandpa that spurred me on to brave the cold and, in this moment, fight a battle not unlike the ones our family had fought many times before. A battle to show some grit and to fight alongside my two brothers and a father figure who realised the importance of quality time and creating memories.

"Pull! Reel! Pull! Reel!" Grandpa began to chant as my brothers joined in. I think for a moment that this was all just blown out of proportion. Standing in the sand, freezing cold with my board shorts and underwear soaked and worm guts mixed with fish guts all over my shirt, I desperately reeled in a rod too heavy for me with the hope that I would land something beyond comprehension. A fish that would get in the local newspaper and be etched in gold lettering on the wall of the local fishing club.

Another almighty bend of the rod and a squeal of the reel shocked me back into focus – the line slowly returned to the reel and my Grandpa reached over to the landing net with both hands firmly grasping the handle. His eyes were wide open, his usual nonplussed expression now alert and slightly afraid.

With more straining came more exhaustion and a loosening of my grip, not on the rod, but my emotions. Tears began to well in my eyes as all the issues of the past few years bubbled to the surface. "It's okay," my brothers said as they saw my shivering body.

"We believe in you," Grandpa would say as he ruffled my hair and we stood there, together.

I furrowed my brow and took a deep breath before using the last of my energy to pull the rod back and reel in, over and over again until the line came in so far that we prepared ourselves to get a first look at the greatest catch of our lives.

It was hard to make out the dark mass slowly moving closer towards us, the crashing waves making it nearly impossible to identify. Instead, we watched in silence as the shadow approached, now worried that it could be a ferocious shark or violent sting ray that was out for vengeance on our innocent toes.

"I'm ready," Grandpa said, bracing himself to swoop the net under the creature.

His body sprang into life as he lunged at our trophy, grunting as he wrangled the beast into the net before pulling it up for us to see.

What beauty, what grace, what . . . nothing.

Not a shimmering tailor or a record-breaking whiting, nor a great white shark or giant squid.

Instead, what Grandpa pulled out of the water was a mass of fishing line tangled around some seaweed. The worm, threaded so carefully around the hook, was untouched and still hanging off the end of the fishing line.

"Well," he said in reply to our dejected faces. "Maybe next time."

And as we looked into the vast expanse of the water in front of us, the endless sand dunes and brightening sky, we knew that there would be a next time. And a time after that. In fact, there would be many years of fishing on Seven Mile Beach, until we grew older and no longer cared for the wonder of waking up so early to catch worms and fish off the beach with Grandpa.

As time marches on, and we grow older and become the teachers to our sons and even grandsons, we'll remember this distant memory with a renewed fondness. We'll realise that moments in the bitter cold with slimy worms threaded through barbed hooks were some of the most cherished moments we shared.

Blood

Christina King

I shared mine with you.
All those months of carrying you around
Inside an ever-growing belly.
My blood was your blood
So your heart could grow.
They gave me needles in case our blood
Types were different.
They weren't.
A pair of negatives together.

And now the needles are yours.
Each time I prick your little finger
You diligently squeeze it,
"A juicy finger, Mum," you'll say
Of the ones that give you a good dollop of the stuff,
A little red bead,
A tiny ruby,
Swelling from the tip of your finger.
We stare at it together,
Just for a moment.
Then it's scooped up by

The machine,
Sucked up, processed,
And a number spat out.
A blood number.
A number created in blood and sugar,
Such a sweet number.
Then another needle, this time in your tummy
To tame the sugar number.

Each time I staple the
Monitor to the back of your arm;
So skinny, your arms
Like a gum sapling's branch.
You try to relax,
Knowing it will hurt all the more if you don't.
We count, we sing, we giggle, we read,
I tell you stories.
And just in the moment, as cruel as it is,
That sweet little moment when you're most relaxed,
I shoot the needle into your arm.
A moment suspended.
With my breath.
Did it hurt?
Sometimes it doesn't and you smile triumphantly.
Sometimes it does and you cry instead.
And sometimes it does hurt, and you smile bravely anyway.
Those times hurt me the most.
Right in my heart,
The factory making my own blood,

Which I would pour into you if I thought it would help.
But it's not my blood you need.

We're always trying to understand what works.
What tames this thing.
This unpredictable, insatiable beast that never sleeps.
This ocean that is constantly changing,
Swirling, shifting, crashing.
And sometimes calm, if only on the surface.

It's only a tiny part of you though.
A mere cloud, scudding past.
It doesn't belong to you, nor you to it.

Your blood was my blood,
But it's your own too.
Just as your story is not my story.
I thought it was, in the early days.
But now you have places to go, things to do.
And you'll take your sweet blood
And your even sweeter heart,
Out into the world,
Find your place there,
And make it better.

My Grandmother's Grandmother

Chloe Isabelle Pryce

My grandmother's grandmother is walking from her rural village into town to sew clothes in the workshop for the rich folk in grand houses in Paris, and her shoes are rubbing, and she's hot in last year's coat – too tight – and

Her grandmother's grandmother is sitting impatiently as an older cousin braids *camomilles sauvages* and *chicorées* into her long hair, and she's dancing in the square to two fiddlers outside the church and her skirt catches on the neighbour's son's boots, twirling, and

Her grandmother's grandmother is shushing the baby and bouncing the baby and calling desperately for her mother-in-law, and shaking the baby and praying he'd start his wretched crying again, or just a single breath, *mon Dieu, mon Dieu*, and

Her grandmother's grandmother is teaching the village girls to move the battered toggles, and it seems like there are hundreds of them jumping and clacking, and her ancient hands flit like tiny wrens and the lace appears, flying like sand through her fingers, and

Her grandmother's grandmother is mixing sage with coriander and wiping cool cloths across her daughters' sweaty brows, muttering to herself and breathing in the thick efflorescent steam, and the fever's been up too long this time, and

Her grandmother's grandmother is kneeling at the stream washing out the bloodied rags with one verse of a love song turning over and over in her mind, and her hands are frigid and quaking and her skin is blue beneath the nails, and her breath is that of a dragon's, and

Her grandmother's grandmother is skinning rabbits, it's always rabbits since the wolves took the goats, and she's in the candlelit corner and the wood is too wet this year and the smoke from the fire is choking and settling in drifts on her greasy apron, and

Her grandmother's grandmother is standing atop the ruined fort with her swollen belly and she's wondering why the herbs did not stop the quickening, and praying that the old woman is right this time, and she is stepping into air, and

Her grandmother's grandmother is emerging from the woods with her skirt mushroom-full and she sees the *arc-en-ciel*, the most vibrant she's ever known, and the morning's rain is clearing and the grass glistens like the rose oil in her sister's bath the day she wed, and

Her grandmother's grandmother is wearing all black, her mother's mourning dress, a widow at nineteen with three hungry babes, and

Her grandmother's grandmother is mouthing out the words carved high and tall on cathedral walls, the ones her father taught her, *SIC ENIM DILEXIT DEUS MUNDUM*, and she has learnt in secret what they mean, that God is indeed good, and loving, and

Her grandmother's grandmother sits atop a cart full of fluttering caged coveys and watches her husband lead the donkey, and the boys are grown quarrelsome and proud these days and wish to be knights and soldiers, and hit at one another with swords made of sticks, and

Her grandmother's grandmother has bright green eyes that do not match her brothers', and she is young yet, and she is dreaming of her own household and quiet and a loom and winter roses, and a husband not often at home, and

Her grandmother's grandmother's grandmother, on and on and on: six thousand grandmothers' lives of love and toil and grief.

I hoist the basket to my hip and walk to the laundromat, podcast about catfishing tinny in one ear

I sit in a square of sunlit courtyard and wipe a vinegary cloth across my leather sandals, to ward off the Sydney damp

I make soup and I sing

I notice the way the yellow evening light hits the neighbour's house, just so, and the shocking pink of the camellias, and the almost-full moon, dangling

I brush out the tangles in my hair and take myself dancing in a tight red dress and white sneakers

I look up at the rain and open my mouth to snatch a taste, bitter and green

I feel lonely

I think of the photograph of my grandmother's grandmother, her stern brow and patchy moustache and enormous stately fur and her jolly third husband

And I wish that she could know me, that my schoolgirl French were better

And for now, I speak into the air:

Je vous vois, grand-mères
Je me souviendrai de vous
Nous sommes toutes pareilles
Nous sommes toutes ici ensembles

See where your efforts have brought us.

Like Two Sides of a Coin

Emoh Ebubechukwu Justina

We as night and day,
agreed on dawn and dusk,
and never anything else.

You fancy owls,
I fancy crows.
You fancy fireflies,
I fancy bees.
You fancy dark clouds,
I fancy blue skies.

Our choices differ,
but we respect each other's
We do not understand,
but we respect.

When I allow the sun to shine too bright
you are always there to save the day
with offerings of your calm moonlight
When you mask the evils committed by night
I will always come by to reveal them in the light

Like two sides of a coin,
We are head and tails
Like two sides of a coin,
we might never see eye-to-eye.
But just like two sides of a coin,
our diversity creates value.
Like two sides of a coin,
we belong as one.

Thus, won't you say,
I hold a place in your soul?
In your very human soul.
Humanity keeping us together,
like two sides of a coin.

Potato Soup

Joshua Marcus

The streets were hot and noisy, like they always were. Ana Romero walked through the thin alleys, past people who lugged carts full of potatoes and watermelons and avocados and beer. Dogs lazed in the sun, their ears twitching whenever the flies that buzzed in circles got too close. A cat leapt from tin roof to bare brick wall to crooked light pole, well clear of the dogs and people below. The smells were a mixture of the pungent wafts of simmering soups, sizzling meats, and piled garbage which rotted in the corners of stairways and the nooks between buildings.

The streets wound their way up and down the mountain slope, a maze of houses and awnings and tarp and small stone steps that turned into slanted walkways and back to steps again. "Don't get lost," Mama always said, and Ana rarely ever did. Since she could walk, Ana had lived, played in and memorised the little winding pathways in the maze. One time when she was five, she had gotten lost and had ended up in someone's living room. The occupant had thought Ana to be a thief and swiped at her with a large broom. That night Mama scolded Ana for the bruise on her forehead, and she hadn't been allowed out of her worried mother's sight for months.

But that was ages ago, and now nine years old, Ana was confident and stronger than she had been. If someone swiped at her with a broom she'd grab it and hit them back with it. Especially if it was some dumb old lady.

Ana slid past a man carrying what looked like wrapped plastic bricks, skirted past a donkey chewing on grass that had sprouted from a crack in the concrete, and climbed the brick wall that gave her access to the rooftops. She snuck her hand into the familiar groove between bricks on the left and used a small electrical box on the right to propel herself to the top of the wall.

Up here Ana could see everything. The sun filled her view and warmed her skin. The streets were noisy and constricting with the clattering of carts and loud music blaring out of windows. From the rooftops she could view the edge of the maze where large buildings sprouted, and beyond that, the beach and ocean. Sunlight caught the tops of waves as they grew taller, approaching the golden line of sand in the distance. Vessels large and small cut through the water while they went about their business, white sails full and taut.

It was also cooler and quiet on the rooftops. The sounds of music and honking vehicles were distant and echoed off the walls, as if Ana was listening through a tube. The wind ruffled her hair and bit her skin as she padded along the rooftops, making sure to keep to the concrete or brick where she could, creeping along the sheet metal where necessary and avoiding the blue or green tarp completely. One time, she had been playing with her neighbour Javier on the rooftops and he slipped and fell through a blue tarp into someone's bedroom. Thankfully, he landed on the bed when no one was home. They had left the sheet to hang in the wind and quickly scampered away laughing, until they saw the first droplets of rain fall from the sky. Both Ana and Javier had felt guilty after that adventure.

Nestled away next to one of the few taller structures in the maze was a small shelter of knee-high brick and a sheet metal roof. In the cluster of buildings and uneven rooftops, it was completely hidden from the streets below and barely noticeable when looking down on it from up the hill. The shelter's roof slanted up so that the open end faced the ocean. Ana loved coming here to watch storms roll in over the bay, imagining giants in the clouds throwing thunderbolts at each other and great beasts of mist and light rumbling in the heights.

As she approached the shelter, a puff of smoke slipped out from underneath the sheet metal roof.

"Mama said that'll kill you, you know," Ana said with a smile, as she ducked under the roof and lay on a thin mattress in the sun. Maria coughed and scowled at her. Ana's older sister was taller and thinner, with jet black hair that tumbled past her shoulder and shimmered in the sunlight.

"I'm fourteen now. I can do what I want," the older girl said, blowing out another plume of smoke. Her big eyes, usually sparkling with mischief, were red and watery.

"You're only smoking because Marcus does," Ana said with a sigh. "And it smells really bad as well. You think they pick stinky people to be in the Carnival parade?"

"I think they pick dancers to be in the Carnival. And all the dancers I know smoke," said Maria, tapping the cigarette onto the concrete next to her. Instead of the usual specks of ash falling, a large black cylinder tumbled out and she had to relight it.

"Like who?" said Ana.

"Like . . . like Juliana Santos, Mama's friend." Maria blew out another plume of smoke and Ana fake coughed.

"Julie's a stripper, not a dancer, idiot."

"She was in the Carnival last year, moron."

"Yeah, and she was naked." Ana rolled her eyes.

"No, she wasn't. She had pants on."

"Whatever," Ana said. Since she could remember, Maria had wanted to be in the Carnival parade, and always used it as an excuse for the questionable things that she did. Ana had no interest in being in Carnival, or any parade for that matter. She wanted to help people, like a doctor, or maybe a vet. There were so many animals in the maze that needed help. "Still doesn't change the fact that you're only smoking because Marcus does."

"I'm smoking because I like it, Ana," Maria said before letting out a muffled cough.

Ana laughed. "Sure, sounds like it."

"Shut up." Maria flicked the cigarette onto the rooftop in front of them. "How's Mama?"

"She's good, just making dinner. We're having potato soup again."

While Ana loved potato soup, this was the third time this week. Ana wanted something filling, like some beef or chicken roasted over hot coals, like the ones they sold at the market. Or maybe some skewers with onions and tomatoes and lamb all stuck together.

"How is her leg?"

"She says it's getting better, but she's still limping," said Ana. "Lucas from next door says it may never properly heal."

"That Lucas doesn't know shit," Maria scoffed as she played with her fingers. "Mama will be back to normal in no time."

Ana doubted that but kept the thought to herself. Just yesterday she had gone with Mama down the hill to walk along the beach. It had taken twice as long to get there and nearly three times as long coming back. It pained Ana to see her Mama hobble up and down the mountainside. Mama's injury prevented her from swimming, which she had previously loved to do at least twice a week. She hadn't said anything, but Ana had seen the expression on Mama's face at the sight of people as they played in the shallows and swam in the deeper water behind the breaking waves. The crystal water had reflected the rays of the sun, nearly blinding Mama.

"Have you heard anything from Carlos?" Ana asked.

"Nothing yet, but he said he'll keep an ear out for information. How many ladies do you think get robbed in this place?"

"I'm not sure."

"It can't be many, Ana. Everyone knows everyone, but Mama said she didn't recognise them. They must have come from a different area."

"I still can't understand why they would do that to Mama, of all people."

"People will do bad things when they're desperate," Maria said, her lips a thin line as she stared into the distance. "There is a lot of desperation at the moment. And a lot of bad things going on. What I don't understand is why they pushed her down the stairs."

"She said that she broke one of their noses."

"But there were three of them. Surely they could have restrained her or just left her. They already had her money," said Maria.

Ana had no answer, but she felt anger bubble inside her as her sister's gaunt face went red. It had been a long two weeks since Mama had been robbed and since then, both sisters had sworn to find the men who had done it. Mama's spirits remained high though and after the first few days of hobbling and cursing, she went back to her normal self. Well, mostly.

While in front of Ana and Maria she joked and laughed, Ana noticed Mama had a new habit of staring out the window, looking at the bustling street with a vacant expression, her hands shaking. Ana had not seen her Mama like this since their Papa had left.

The only memories Ana had from that time four years ago were lots of yelling, a slamming door and Mama sobbing uncontrollably for nearly a week. Once Mama had been able to speak again, she had said to both girls that Papa was never coming back, and he hadn't. Neither Ana or Maria had been given a proper explanation as to why and whenever they raised the topic Mama cursed under her breath and walked away. Maria thought that maybe he had not been faithful, though Ana found that difficult to believe. She still hoped that one day she would come home and Papa would be there to greet her, happy and smiling.

"You still haven't told me what we'll do if we find them," Ana said, glancing at her sister, who was deep in thought. Initially she had been all for taking revenge on three full-grown adults, but the idea got scarier the more she thought about it.

"I'll think of something." Maria's voice was distant as she lit another cigarette. "Wait, did you hear that?" The older girl sat upright, suddenly alert.

"What?" Ana said, intrigued.

"Shh . . . just listen." Maria put a finger to her lips and closed her eyes, Ana did the same.

In the distance, cars spluttered and horns honked. Closer, Ana heard chatter, people bartering in the nearby markets. Some voices high and raised, others muffled and distant. But there was one voice that cut through them all, loud and nasal, speaking English.

Ana opened her eyes and saw Maria's lips part into a smile. "Americans," Ana said.

"Do you want to be the distraction, or the lifter?" said Maria. Her eyes were wide as she took another drag of her cigarette. This time she didn't cough.

"You're too old to be the distraction anymore," Ana said. "Remember last time? Those English people didn't even give you a second glance when you asked to speak to them."

"So that means I'm the lifter."

"I think I can do both."

"What do you mean?" Maria narrowed her eyes and pursed her lips.

"I mean my hands are smaller than yours, and . . ."

"And what?" Maria said.

"And last time you nearly got caught." Ana looked at the bare concrete on the roof in front of them. It was never easy to tell Maria her shortcomings, but usually her older sister got over it quickly. Especially if there was money involved.

"Yeah, but I didn't."

"That's because they were drunk, and it was dark. You're also forgetting that they nearly caught me."

"I know that," said Maria, pondering over it. Ana had always been the better lifter, though she would never say that in front of her sister. Maria was often too clunky and focused on speed, she didn't have the soft touch that Ana did. Taking wallets out of the pockets of tourists was an art, and while Ana was still young enough to get away with manipulating dumb foreigners into feeling bad for her, she planned to make the most of it.

"Last week I got an Australian wallet all by myself, while you were at school." Ana sat upright. "I can do it, trust me."

Maria took a drag and rolled the smoke around her mouth, eventually blowing it out into the wind. "I don't want you going down there by yourself."

"Well, you can come and watch if you want. And I'll still split it fifty-fifty."

"Alright," Maria's voice was uncertain. "We'd better hurry before they leave."

They left the shelter and scampered across the rooftops to the next street, where they climbed down a crooked electrical post and into the madness of the markets. Rows and rows of colourful spices and dried fruits and nuts lined alleyways that were covered with felt awnings. Some shops sold knock off bags and sunglasses, while others sold fresh fruit that they crushed into juices. Ana's favourite was watermelon juice with ice in it, a perfect treat after a hot day of climbing over the rooftops. And it was always sweeter after stealing a wallet from an unsuspecting foreigner. She could taste it already.

The high nasal voice was nearly thunderous down here, and Ana and Maria followed the sound until they saw a middle-aged couple speaking in English to a local, who was presumably their tour guide. Ana nearly laughed when she saw what they were wearing. They had tried their hardest to dress casually and blend in but had failed miserably. The man wore three quarter length cargo pants and a colourful t-shirt, while the woman wore a white singlet and a frilly dress that was the exact same as the sundresses they sold three streets over. The real giveaways though, if that wasn't enough, were the expensive sunglasses and baseball caps. Ana had only ever seen tourists in the maze wear hats like that. At least these idiots had the sense to not wear watches and jewellery, but that wouldn't be enough to save their wallets.

"Left side," Maria said as they walked past the tourists. The tour guide was talking to the owner of the shop as the two Americans surveyed the selection of cheap leather bags and shoes. Ana glanced at the left pocket of the man's pants and saw the familiar square outline. A rush of nerves and energy prickled her spine, but she didn't show it. She wanted to prove to Maria how easily she could do it. In truth, the Australian last week had realised straight away that his wallet was missing. Ana had been lucky to wriggle free and scamper up a nearby pole onto the rooftops, something she'd never tell Maria.

Ana peeled off from Maria and circled back around to where the couple was. They were talking loudly between each other about the price of the goods. Quiet as a mouse, she padded behind them and tapped the woman on the shoulder.

"Hola señora," Ana said. She angled her face down but kept her eyes up and gave the woman a big toothy smile.

"Oh my god! David, look at her. Isn't she adorable?" The woman's face split into a wide smile. "She looks just like Jackie's girl, don't you think?" The man turned around, his pale face quivering in the heat.

"Do you have food, mister and madame?" Ana asked in broken English. While she could speak English quite well, Ana found this strategy worked a lot better.

"I suppose we can spare a sandwich, Deb." The man huffed as he opened the bag. Ana took the sandwich and put on her biggest smile, allowing her eyes to sheen over like she was about to cry.

"Gracias, my friends!" Ana gave the woman a hug and switched the sandwich from her right hand into her left hand. Since the wallet was in the man's left pocket, she decided to use her right hand. Ana broke free of the hug and jumped into the unsuspecting arms of the man.

"Oh lord how cute!" the lady squealed as she pulled out her phone to take a photo. The man stumbled under Ana's weight, and as that happened, she slid her hand into his left pocket and wrapped her fingers around the small leather case. Quickly slipping it into her own shorts, she jumped off.

"Gracias again, friends!" Ana said as she hurried away through the crowd.

"I taught you well, little one." Maria appeared, beaming. Just as she said this, Ana heard a shout from behind them. "We had better get back to the rooftops."

"Lead the way," Ana said. Her breaths were short and excited, fingers curled tight around her prize.

Behind one of the many fruit shops there was a little courtyard filled with bins. Ana hated the courtyard because of the smell, but the ladder there was the easiest way to get back on the rooftops. Once up and out of the madness, the cries of the Americans were a distant memory, and the sisters made their way back towards the shelter.

"What's in there, Ana?" Maria asked, still smiling. They sat on the mattress and sifted through the wallet.

"Woah! A lot of money," said Ana. "Driver's license, bank card, some paper, not sure what this is . . ." Ana pulled out what looked like a tiny donut sealed in plastic.

Maria laughed. "You won't need any of that, toss it. How much money is there?"

While the random crap from the wallet ended up down the small void between buildings, Ana counted out the cash and coins. "We have R$252."

"Not a bad catch," Maria said. "Not as good as that time when we scored over a thousand, but not bad."

"That was years ago. They don't carry as much cash anymore. Carlos says they're getting smarter as well."

"Maybe Carlos is just getting worse," Maria laughed.

"You'd know what that feels like, don't you?"

"Shut up," the older girl said. "We'll wait a little bit for the Americans to leave, then go down and buy some stuff. How's that sound?"

Ana nodded in agreement. Over the next hour or so, the sun drifted lower and lower towards the waterline. The light reflected off clouds and rolling waves, sending beams of velvet and turquoise and lilac into the air. The birds flew around the shelter and scampered on the roof in playful jest, and the noise of the market grew while people went about their evening shop. Ana watched boats catch gusts of wind and skim across the surface of the water. Maria played tricks with her lighter as she smoked.

Once the sky had faded to near darkness, the sisters emerged from the shelter and went back to the markets. With her newfound wealth, Ana bought them both watermelon juice, at the cost of R$40. Maria looked at nice dresses and bags and shoes, while Ana looked at tea pots and decorative bowls. Steam from large vessels rose into the air and coiled under the faded tarps, the fragrant aroma masking the foul street odours that had arisen with the heat of the day.

Ana walked past a simmering pot full of meat and thought about the potato soup they were going to have for dinner when she saw a table of ornate pipes and knives. The handles and hilts had plastic gems and ringlets of steel that had been painted gold. While ornate, the pipes looked clean enough for actual use and the knives sharp enough to slice and cut.

Maria appeared next to her, eyes glimmering from the sheen of the fake gold and silver.

"Aren't they beautiful? Even if they are fake," the older sister said. "Look at that one, with the big emerald in the hilt. Wouldn't that be great to bring home to Mama?"

"I think Mama would appreciate a knife with a more comfortable handle," Ana said with a smile. "But maybe we should get some meat."

A man appeared in front of them, with a great belly that stretched the cotton shirt tight across his front. His chins wobbled as he spoke and his eyes glimmered. "Only R$200 for you, beautiful ladies. Very good quality, made by the finest blacksmiths in the country. But if you want something a little fancier . . . you see this one here, they say a sultan himself used this to slay his enemies. And this one was driven into the black heart of a dragon back in the Middle Ages, if you believe such things."

Ana giggled. Next to her, Maria leaned back, crossed her arms, and pouted her lips.

"How much for the dragon slayer?" said Maria.

"Usually R$400, but for you little lady I will make it 300." The man smiled. "Only because one day you will grow up and make a man very happy, maybe my son, eh? And give them many beautiful children." He took a step back and did as low a bow as his large figure would allow, which was not very low.

"So you'll give me a dragon slaying dagger for R$300?" Maria said, a smile creeping over her face. "I'm not so sure, dragon slaying is only worth R$250 in my books. What about sea monsters? Do you have any weapons here that have killed sea monsters?"

"No, however I do have a spear out the back that belonged to Blackbeard." The man smirked. "But maybe smart girls like yourselves don't want ancient and powerful weapons such as these."

Maria uncrossed her arms and narrowed her eyes. "What about real weapons?" she said. Ana's chest tightened, and she wanted to shake Maria, to snap her out of whatever crazy thought that had entered her mind. But it was too late.

"Girls such as yourselves have no need of real weapons."

"Girls such as ourselves know what we need and what we don't," Maria said. "Do you have any?"

The man's squashed face turned red. "Will these girls tell me what they can afford in the category of real weapons?" Ana's eyes darted back and forth between the man and Maria. She was too nervous to talk. They should have been buying food, not weapons.

"We have R$200." Maria replied. The man's laughter was thunderous and booming.

"Why my dears, you cannot buy any weapons with that." The man moved to turn away.

"We don't want guns," Maria said, desperate. "Something a little less lethal, like a knife, or . . ."

"Hmm, maybe I do have something for you," the man turned back. "Very popular among my female customers." He reached a chubby hand underneath the table and pulled out a small black canister. It reminded Ana of a deodorant can. "Pepper spray for you, perhaps?"

"That could work." Maria said. She reached for the canister, but the man pulled it away.

"Money first," he said.

"How much did you say? One hundred, was it?" Maria said, playing dumb. The man let out a fake laugh.

"R$300," he spat. Ana wanted the man to stay at the price of 300, something they could certainly not afford, but she knew he would come down. And she knew how good Maria was at haggling.

Maria laughed. "R$300! That's the same price as the dragon slaying dagger." A scowl crossed the man's face. "150."

"250 is the lowest I will go, little lady," the man said, his chins wobbling in the dim light. "This is real pepper spray, and not some decorative toy."

"170." Maria pouted.

"250." The man stood firm and went to place the canister back behind the table.

"Alright, alright," Maria said. "200. And if someone asks how we came into possession of such a weapon, we'll say we found it on the street, forgetting all about your little stall in the market."

The man huffed and Ana glanced over to her sister, who crossed her arms and had a smirk on her face.

"Fine," the man said, seemingly disgusted by the way Maria had haggled with him. "But you better not come back here again, or you'll be sorry." The man glanced at Ana. "That goes for you as well, little one." Ana's face went red and she looked at the ground. Making enemies with adults was not something that she wanted to make a habit of. Now that they had pepper spray, that might not be so easy.

After the exchange, they both scampered back to the rooftop shelter. Giddy with excitement, Maria turned the can over in her hand. "Now if we find the people who hurt Mama, we have a way to hurt them back," she said.

"Are you . . . are you sure that's a good idea?" Ana said in a soft tone. Her stomach growled and pangs of hunger brought her mind back to the simmering pots full of meat at the markets.

"What do you mean?" Maria snapped.

"I mean even if we do find them, they're adults. You saw how easy it would have been to buy a gun today if we had more money."

"Ana, look at me. Do you want those people who hurt Mama to just walk around every day, free from the consequences of their actions? How many other old ladies do you think they will rob and hurt, or worse?"

"I just meant that we should think –"

"What if next time, they throw someone down a set of stairs and kill them?" Maria's face was crimson and her eyes were wide. A small slither of guilt ran up Ana's neck. "If you don't want to help me, fine. I'll do it myself. But remember one thing, Ana. We don't live in a nice place. Maybe it seems nice to you now, but when you get older, you'll realise that it's unforgiving. We live in a place where ladies can be robbed without fear of consequences. Where anyone can buy weapons for the right amount of money. Where stealing is normal and even rewarded." Ana looked down at her shoes as her sister continued. "If you let people walk over you and do whatever they want, you'll be crushed. Mama can't go out and find those people herself because they busted her leg, but we can and we have to. What if they come back and break her other leg? Or what if they do it to us, or one of our friends?" Maria was nearly hysterical now, a clear film over her eyes. Ana felt tears run down her own face, though she did not sob or splutter. "So what'll it be, Ana?"

Ana did not answer straight away. Guilt, anger, confusion all swirled in her head like a storm. She was angry at her sister for making her feel this way. Angry at the people that hurt Mama. Angry at her mama for fighting back instead of letting them walk away with her money. "I – I guess I'm with you." Ana sighed. It was the right thing to do. "Of course I am."

Maria shuffled next to Ana, hugged her and kissed the top of her head. Ana felt her sister's tears fall onto her hair. "We take care of each other, right. We have to."

The heat of the day was starting to dissipate as the last rays of the sun slipped behind the horizon. A shiver went up Ana's spine. "Always," she said. "Always." She felt Maria sag into her arms. The large frame of her sister was heavy but Ana did not mind. After a time, Ana wiped her eyes and stroked Maria's hair.

"Nearly time for some dinner, I think," Ana said. "Mama is probably wondering where we are."

"You're right," Maria said. Her face was dark and puffy, and she coughed. "Time to go home."

As they clambered over the rooftops up the hill, many thoughts ran through Ana's head. Would a single can of pepper spray even be enough for three full grown men? Maybe they could get Marcus to help them, or maybe they could get more cans of pepper spray if they had luck tricking more tourists.

Ana thought about Mama alone at home preparing dinner for Maria and her and tears formed in the corners of her eyes. Maybe one day she'd find a tourist's wallet full of money to buy them all a nice place outside of the maze, where people didn't get hurt or robbed. Where they didn't need to spend their money on weapons but could buy fresh meat and fish for dinner. Or maybe one day she'd become a famous vet and they could live in a big house with the animals that Ana had saved, surrounded by dogs and cats and mice that loved them and played with them every day.

These thoughts left Ana's mind as she walked through the front door and smelled dinner. Her stomach rumbled and Mama greeted them with a wide smile.

"Welcome home my girls," Mama said. "Keeping out of trouble? Dinner is nearly ready."

"Just out doing some shopping," said Maria. "Marcus got paid at his new job yesterday so he bought us some juice."

"You smell like cigarettes." Mama sniffed the air with suspicion and Ana had to use all of her effort to not smirk.

"Marcus smokes, you know that Mama," said Maria. "I won't touch the stuff. You know they wouldn't pick a smelly person to be in Carnival."

Ana smiled and nodded. "It was just Marcus." There was no point telling Mama the truth about the smoking, because Maria would instantly tell the truth about where they got the money for the juice and then they'd both be in trouble.

"How is your leg, Mama?" asked Ana.

"It's been a lot better today." Mama grimaced as she turned and went to pull the pot off the burner to bring to the small plastic table.

"No you don't," said Maria as she grabbed the pot from Mama's hands and brought it to the table. Ana saw Mama purse her lips but her eyes gave away that she was relieved.

"You *do* smell like smoke, Maria. Were you kissing Marcus?" Mama hobbled over to the table and the three of them sat.

Maria rolled her eyes and Ana fake gagged. "We're just friends alright, no kissing. And no smoking, at least for me."

"Alright, you are too young for that anyway," said Mama. "Please start girls, before it goes cold."

Maria served three bowls of potato soup and the familiar wafts of rosemary, ginger and garlic filled Ana's nose. The smell made her forget about the markets, the stolen wallet, the pepper spray and Mama's injury, as it poured through the room, surrounding them. Ana was so hungry, she didn't even

mind it was the third time this week that Mama had cooked
potato soup.

Let Me Be the Mountain

Chloe Isabelle Pryce

my love is like the stone's for water
as old as time, and
unending as the sky.
earth sign, earthbound,
my heart seeks solace
in the cool embrace
of seafoam and streamlets and storm.

I have loved the river and the sea
I have been tumbled
and cracked in two.
I have been shrunk to nothing,
my edges made smooth and dull in time.
my love has ever sought to be immersed,
to be moulded by the object
of its passions,
to be altered forever by what it adores.

I have loved the rain
that drop by drop
made tear tracks on my skin,
that slowly and kindly
turned a creek to a crevasse.
my love has ever sought that tender kiss,
that balm which cannot heal
and cannot stay,
for what downpour ever quenched
the bedrock's thirst?
instead it carved out caverns in my heart,
left me hollow, and brittle,
and dry as driftwood.

if I must be made of stone,
let me be the mountain.

if I must love the water,
let me love the spring.

let my love rise from deep within.
let it not seek to break
or cast me down.
let it be pure, and cold,
and life-bringing:
let flowers and grasses flourish
where it flows across my weathered back.
let us be one, the spring and the mountain.
let us watch the world together from our peak.
let us know entirely who we are.

let us remember how we rose
like giants from the sea,
how the waves receded
and the sun beat down like joy.
let us remember
how the shells and ammonites
within our bones
stood high enough at last
to never feel the rain.

Evening Walks Along the Sunbird Circle

Sanskriti Satyakam

On most evenings of the weekdays, my mother and I take a stroll along the narrow streets of the Sunbird Circle; a quiet neighbourhood in the far eastern region of Singapore, with jumbo duplexes arranged circularly, facing a beautiful lush green park where the sight of sunbirds is quite common, hence the name Sunbird Circle. The gleaming windows of the fancy cars that look like they have never been driven make my mum's eyes look moss green. I wonder if my eyes look that pretty in the sun.

Something about these lanes feels like the ones outside my grandmother's house in the suburbs of olden Delhi, maybe they are also fed the same dosage of sunlight each late noon. Walking along the Sunbird Circle almost always makes me wish it was winter and I could enter through one of the gigantic gates of these sun-kissed homes and walk straight into the woolen-sleeved arms of my grandmother, expecting *masala chai* to make its way to me at the end of the hug and my *nani* cosying me up with a soft shawl around me as I take the warm cup in my cold hands.

The rectangular, black granite name plate embedded on the wall of one of the houses located at the entrance of the Sunbird locality reads "Brig. Gen. Tiwari", another stark similarity between my maternal grandmother's home and this one. My late grandfather served in the Indian army as a Brigadier General and happens to have the same last name, Tiwari. I wonder if this house smells like someone's childhood too. Or if when its doorbell rings, kids rush outside expecting their parents to be home from work. Just like my cousins would when I rang the doorbell and peeped through the space between the two closed gates with wide eyes, waiting for them to scream my name so I could scream theirs and fill the air with the sound of our much awaited reunion. Together we would race to my grandfather's room hoping to get the TV remote first so we could play *Ninjajinja* (the only video game we had installed on our TV).

Just as my mother and I increase our walking pace, we are met by strangers (who we have often exchanged smiles with before) walking or jogging in the opposite direction. A tall girl with neon-orange coloured Nike shoes and black gym leggings has her hair tied in a high ponytail that swings from side to side as she jogs. I hear Ed Sheeran's "Photograph" playing through her headphones as she jogs past us. I wonder why one would play a slow song like that while jogging and not Måneskin's "Beggin". Don't most people listen to songs that are upbeat, peppy and fast-rhythmed while working out? But then again how can I question her song selection for a jog when I myself listen to Mohit Chauhan's "Tum Se Hi" sometimes on the treadmill.

At a slight distance I see a canopy that has a terracotta shingled roof, right amidst the Sunbird Park. Usually, the little wooden benches inside it are unoccupied when I come for walks here. However, today I see a middle-aged man sitting on the bench at the centre with his legs folded and arms on his knees. From a distance, it looks like he has surrendered himself to the lush green arms of this beautiful park and his chin is held high as if he is trying to hug the rays of the setting sun that are making their way to the canopy through the trees. As we come closer, I see his eyebrows are lowered and pulled closer together making wrinkles appear on his forehead. His cheeks look red as if he has cried and I start to wonder if he is sad or worried.

"He is sitting exposed to the world that he is worried by, to master the art of not being worried by it," I think to myself to make sense of his shrunken face.

On the other hand, I see a little baby, probably just six months old, widened eyes glancing over the entire Sunbird Circle, occasionally turning her head to see if her mother is still the one strolling her stroller. As the mother-daughter duo come closer to mine, I see the baby lean back and rest against the stroller seat and smile at me as though everything has been taken care of and there is nothing in the world to worry about. Then the baby turns around to confirm her mother's presence which she fears will vanish, just like the type of confirmation the man meditating must be seeking in his meditative state – a safe place he trusts to topple and tumble into when pushed by the worries of the world.

The wind at this time of the day is usually not as cool as it gets later in the evening. My mother, who is not dressed in traditional jogging wear, has her hair open and it brushes against her face every now and then because we're walking in the opposite direction to the wind. She tucks a strand behind her ears and looks at me, pointing at the right side to the dog (probably of the American Eskimo breed) who is poking his fluffy face out from between the two metal rods of the gate. Knowing my immense love for dogs, my mother expects me to rush to pet the dog so she slows down as we reach the gate.

And as expected, I run to the dog, stretching my right arm into the space between the rods and over its head to caress his soft scalp as he fastens his wags. As I kneel down to level my face with the dog's, I see the door behind him open and a boy probably in his early teens looks at me and smiles. I take his smile as an approval for me to continue petting the dog. I wave from a distance and he widens his smile but does not respond to my greeting, shutting the door slightly and walking back into the house. The dog's wag-pace is now so high that I start to think that it has never been played with before and was longing for the warmth that it is receiving from me. Was he just their status symbol?

"So cute!" says my mother who is still standing a little far from the gate. I force myself to turn away from the dog and join my mother as we both equally fasten our pace, aware of the setting sun. As we near the exit, my eyes still keep eagerly scanning the gates of other houses we pass by; in search of another dog I could quickly pet to satisfy my forever-dog-loving heart. The Sunbird Circle is my favourite piece of Singapore because it radiates the essence of India I knew as a child. Because it allows me to weave my thoughts, leave them there, come back and weave some more. Because just like many other incompletely woven pieces of thoughts that I left in many other places I could probably never go back to again, Sunbird Circle will home these. Always.

Train Travel

Dennis Haskell

As a small child in Sydney
like others, my family
had little money, and no car,
so we often caught the train.
Those staid, dark red carriages
ranted and swayed and rattled
as if arguing with the rails.

On rare occasions
we would go all the way to town
past curious, unknown suburbs,
past hedges strangely cut
into unnatural shapes: cars, trees,
a spectacular Harbour Bridge.

I was spellbound
how after frantic, thronging Central
the train went from daylight into night,
noise exaggerated and fussed about:
most doors were held open then
and all the darkness rushed in

until you burst into sunlight
spread on the dazzling Harbour
unspeakably beautiful below.

If you fell, death was waiting
but dying didn't share my world
back then; I was more
fascinated than frightened

but if you stayed on the train
you entered the darkness again.

Nineteen views of Itsukushima

Nicholas Osiowy

I
Appendix of the liver-country,
I swim slowly and send her to
Agony: my gills are locked
If you could see them still.

II
It had to be – the closing swans
Over the bay, with wings green
From sacred roosts. This is where
They lie – happiness in death.

III (Anatta)
No matter how they toss the dice
No "I" can be, no we. With
Swans, we fly free and realise
The black pit of our plumage.

IV
Imagine plum trees, gently blown
Over ridges, down mountains
To our home – where nightingale song
Already moves me.

V
Shrine in tide-web:
A line of tourists
Disappearing to the horizon.

VI
Floating torii,
A line of tourists
Broken wood sinking.

VII
Moss on a shrine roof:
Mould to the lazy sea,
So full of points to make.

VIII
Red armpitted pagoda
Nuzzling me in a storm:
My kid-fur has not moulted!

IX
Even here I am bored,
As if it were a writer's house
With school desk and warm wine.

X
I desire what I am not;
I pilot beneath
A Japanese fin.

XI
Marigolds with wet hands;
Brightly green they cup
Their morning faces with worry.

XII
My hat is brown with grime;
A doe sniffs in disgust and a
Buck wants to eat it.

XIII
A loud waterfall drowns
Voices, but the high tide of guilt
Aches the rocky hinge of my knee.

XIV
At the base of Mount Misen
With umbrella and shirt
As a diver with tube and trunks.

XV
Though June covers Misen
With her wet sheets,
Their flapping trudges its paths.

XVI
Alone in a wood,
I recite memories of books
And manufacture poetry.

XVII
Like the gannet my pen
Slices through white hills
With a yellow band of memory.

XVIII
Like a seducer, my cough
Comes at my bed and flees
To the pouring rain when I am alone.

XIX
Green's light is nourished
In its turning colour;
In the grove of maples
Is the dust of stars.

Next Door

Sarah Nielsen

Sometime that first week, I caught Weiying at her front door, umbrella propped on her shoulder, one of her kids next to her, bedraggled. I wasn't going to stop – we were nod-and-smile neighbours – but I hesitated and raised my hand as my kids ran inside. She waved me over and shouted over the rain, "So good for the gardens!"

"Yes!" I wasn't sure what to say so I pointed to my feet. "I had to buy gumboots!"

"Me too!" She stuck out a gumbooted foot and waggled it at me. I laughed and she laughed back. The kid rolled her eyes and went inside, leaving us talking over the space between our front doors, raising our voices over the sound of the rain streaming over the front verandah and washing down the footpath.

The rain continued all that week and the next. I walked the kids to school with my big umbrella. Joey was full of jitters, jumping into the rushing gutters, water sloshing over the top of her gumboots. Luca asked to hold the umbrella and he hoisted it aloft, sinewy arms extended to get it over my head. He told me about all the new notices stuck up at school: the floors are very slippery. No running. No running. NO RUNNING!

One morning, we saw Weiying's eldest struggling with her umbrella at the front gate. Luca invited her to walk with us.

"She's called Kaya, Mum! She's in year six." We brought her into our huddle and overlapped our umbrellas as a phalanx against the rain.

"Is that okay?" Weiying was at her front door, dressed for work, her youngest on her hip.

"Of course, the more the merrier!"

"Rain, rain, go away," yelled the three kids, already in unison. "Come again some other day!"

Weiying's daughter seemed happy to talk to Luca despite the two-year age gap. She peppered him with questions about his old school, the kids in his class, his views on handball. Joey trotted to keep up, hanging on the big kid conversation. For the first time since they started, the kids left me at the gate without hesitating. I walked back home to work, to my co-workers in little squares on my computer monitor.

Late one Sunday afternoon, Weiying and her husband knocked on my door and offered to take the kids for a muddy walk. He introduced himself (call me Jay) and their toddler (this is Sammy). Jay had Sammy in a plastic-wrapped pram. Kaya was yellow-raincoated and swinging on our gate. The clouds had cleared and a burst of sun hit the footpath, making it steam. "We're already taking our lot out. Two more won't make a difference."

"Yes please!" The kids left without being asked twice. I could hear their voices fade out down the street, Joey's piping high as she sang her new favourite song. For a moment, I had the house to myself, quiet except for a pattering on the roof as the rain started again. I looked out the window and let the green of the backyard slip out of focus.

By then, the gardens were growing wild and huge with all the water. Tradescantia tendrils snaked across the grass towards my vegetable patch, no matter how quickly I ripped them back. The branches of the trees hung low and heavy and violently green. It felt like a different climate; we were spun into a tropical zone with explosive growth and steamy damp.

When Weiying and Jay handed back the kids after the walk, Luca was bursting with news. At the park, one of the hundred-year-old fig trees had tipped then sank to the ground. The council closed the oval with flapping orange tape. Luca and Kaya talked over each other racing to tell me the story of the tree, the tape, the oval. "We'll walk to the other park, next time," said Jay.

Weiying said sotto voce, "It's so sad. The birds were screeching and screeching."

"Mum!" Joey tugged at the leg of my trousers and I looked down to her upturned face. "The birds were crying, Mum, 'cause the tree was their home and now it's gone." She wrapped her arms around my legs and leaned into me. Weiying gave me a half smile and mouthed, "Sorry."

One drizzly evening, I passed Weiying a couple of fallen lemons over the fence between our backyards. She stood on a bucket to get a better look, leaning on the fence, peeking out from the hood of her raincoat. "What's happening in your lovely garden?"

The garden was my solace. I made a vegetable patch in every place I rented. I had only just got this one started before the rain. I didn't have the words to explain all this so I shrugged. "Such a mess! The tomatoes split before I could get to them. One day they were green, the next day . . ." I mimed an explosion. We both looked at the veggie bed, full of boisterous growth that had collapsed under its own weight.

It was around then, after a particularly big storm, that the sewers bubbled and slowly, majestically overflowed. Everything stopped for a while as trucks double-parked in the street with digging equipment and flashing lights. I saw Weiying at the supermarket next to the shelf of damp catchers. There were only two left. I handed her one.

"There is literal shit in the street!" She had the wide-eyed, amused look that we all had at that time.

"I know, so much drama; the sewers are full of wipes!"

We left together. It was comforting to walk with another adult, talking about nothing much, our shopping bags swinging.

Weiying was curious about the rain in a way that I wasn't. She told me all about the different types of storms and the names for all the clouds. I had avoided learning anything. I told myself there wasn't much time in between work and the kids and the whole new layer of domestic labour brought by the rain – the endless trying to clean things and dry things. But really it was a type of anti-curiosity; I didn't want to know, I just wanted it to go away. I felt a quick beat of embarrassment.

She was still talking, but now seemed to draw to a conclusion. "It might last a long time."

I turned to her and looked under her umbrella. Her face was creased.

"Well, at least we have damp catchers," I said. Too flippant, but she slipped her arm in mine and we walked home that way.

It took a lot longer than anyone anticipated to clean up the sewage. You could smell it underneath the tang of rain and wetness. Every morning, Weiying brought Kaya out to meet us for the walk to school. "Good, smelly morning," I called. Joey giggled and Luca sighed, "Muuuuum". But Weiying always laughed.

She would say, "Thanks for this."

I would flap my hand to ward it off. "No problem." The kids would walk along, holding their noses, honking and laughing.

The water settled into the walls and floors, and they became sticky with the moisture. The paint in our lounge room bubbled like a large blister. When I pushed it with my finger, I could feel the water behind it. At night, the air was thick and musty, and when I crawled into bed, the sheets were spongy. It didn't make for restful sleep and I felt sharp edged with tiredness.

I shouted at Luca after I stepped on a piece of Lego, irritation fizzing. His face was startled blank and my mood dropped immediately. "I just need a bit of help, okay?"

He tracked across the floor on hands and knees, picking up his Lego one brightly coloured brick at a time until he reached me and threw himself at my knees. We both said sorry, sorry, sorry. "I'll help you, Mum," he said.

Weiying came over while I was cooking dinner and asked to borrow some flour; hers had gone mouldy. There was a storm that night and the windows rattled with the wind. "Our roof is leaking," she said. She took the container of flour I gave her and hugged it to her chest. "We can't even get someone to come and look at it. I am so . . . ugh."

I looked up at the dark, damp bruises on my kitchen ceiling. "Yeah, I know the feeling."

Weiying laughed quick and hard and I found myself laughing too, until both of us were leaning on the kitchen counter, wiping our teary eyes. When she left, I handed her the last of the good tomatoes. The next day, she brought me muffins for my morning tea.

Soon after, the electricity went out in our part of the city. There were promises of a quick repair, but that didn't happen. The kids were sent home from school, so I tried to work from the lounge room, stepping over toys and craft materials in between making sandwich after sandwich. I rationed the apples to one a day to stop the kids eating them all from boredom.

In the evenings, the shadows came in quickly without streetlights. Joey didn't like the dark and the way it made things unfamiliar. She kept close to me, my little talkative shadow. I moved her mattress into my bedroom so I could be there if she woke in the absolute darkness of the night. My mother rang and suggested we go stay with her in Queensland. "You never should have left," she said. "It would be so much easier if you weren't living in another state."

I told her we were settled here. I said leaving felt like an overreaction. Surely the power would click back on soon?

Weiying knew someone down the road with solar panels, so we gathered up all our devices and took them over to charge. She lugged a bag filled with plugs and cables and a power board so she could plug everything in at once.

"Good thinking," I said. "What would I do . . ."

"Without me?" she laughed and jostled my arm, weighed with the bag of phones and iPads.

We ate up everything in the fridge and freezer. The kids and I made a camp kitchen with the barbeque on the back verandah. I liked standing out there in the mornings making breakfast while Weiying did the same over the fence. "Morning. Porridge today!" she would call and I would offer cinnamon.

It was not so nice cooking dinner as the light dimmed and the night closed in, but I had the comfort of Weiying doing the same just there. One night, we made a large pot of cocoa, enough for kids and adults, and we all sat around my kitchen table to drink it. Jay found some marshmallows at the back of their pantry. Joey was happier after that night – the cocoa made the dark friendly, she said.

The week after the power went out, I walked to the shops on a day when the rain was light. A damp mist clung around the lower streets, turning the world opaque. When I got to the supermarket it was a new place – empty shelves where there had once been colour and abundance. There were no apples, no bananas, no eggs. When I went to collect the kids from Weiying's I asked if she had eggs. I wanted to make pancakes in the morning.

"Sorry, I haven't had any for days."

The kids were spaced around her loungeroom building a city from blocks under camping lights and candles. A long line of mould had spread down the wall from a hole in the ceiling.

Weiying crossed her arms, hugging herself. "I wish I knew how long this is going to last." I didn't know if she meant the empty supermarket, the power outage, or the rain – likely she meant all of it.

I patted her arm and she cupped her hand over mine. "I'm so glad we have you next door," she said.

"And I'm so glad I have you." The words slipped out easily.

We started sharing meals, passing plates and bowls over the fence. If I made lentil soup, she cooked flatbread; if she cooked sausages, I baked potatoes. The day was bracketed by one of us collecting the devices to charge up the road and the other going to the shops to see what there was to be had. Jay was still travelling into work and brought home things from the city. One day he brought home apples, half a dozen straining the sides of his work backpack. The kids ate them all in one afternoon and we didn't stop them. Joey was so thrilled she danced a celebration on the verandah while we clapped and sang to accompany her. Weiying had a sweet singing voice and knew all the words to my kids' favourite Taylor Swift songs.

The electricity went on, then off again, and stayed off. The outage spread over the power company map that I checked on my phone. Soon the whole city was dark at night. It was a different place without lights, smaller, our world shrunk to local streets. We were all at home all the time; there was nowhere to go. We pried a couple of palings off the fence to make a doorway between the backyards. The big kids formed a tight pack, roaming between our houses depending on where the food was or where the adults were working. I stopped locking the doors. I realised one dinnertime that I hadn't heard a car in the street or a plane in the sky all day. All I could hear was the sound of playing children and the drip and gurgle of the rain overflowing the gutters. I stopped thinking about taking the kids to Queensland; it felt unfathomably far away. There was only *here*.

Weiying helped me hang solar fairy lights on my front fence and hers so we could find our homes in the dark street. We wound them around the metal posts, pushing the dense grevillea growth back into the front garden bed.

"How are you going?" Her voice was low. We were standing close, under the front verandah, watching the tiny, hopeful lights flicker on as the afternoon dimmed.

"Okay." Because despite it all, I was. She slid her arm around my shoulder. Such a small gesture of comfort. We stood together watching the rain, waiting for it to end.

The Cat Upstairs

Chloe Isabelle Pryce

I never see the cat upstairs
but I hear him,
his tiny feet clattering,
patterning the floorboards
over my head.

I never see the neighbours,
but I know them
by their octopus hanger on the line;
know her socks and his scrubs,
and their favourite colours –
turquoise, mauve.

Today the upstairs cat is calling –
his little voice cries out
across a rare quiet moment,
quiet enough that I might hear.

The sheets are cool, damp corridors,
the concrete's warm.
I breathe, and my skin
observes the breeze,
my fingertips the dew collected

like jewels along the clothesline,
like icicles under the eaves.

I am alive,
and so is the cat upstairs –
and so the world turns.

About the Authors

Johnny Banh

I am studying to be an English and History teacher at the University of Sydney. I live in Western Sydney.

Samantha Bowers

I am a writer, teacher and former lawyer living and working in Sydney on unceded Darramuragal and Gadigal lands. I hold a Master of Creative Writing and am completing a Creative Writing PhD at the University of Sydney, exploring the domestic violence crisis through fiction. My journalism has been published in *The Sydney Morning Herald* and *Australian Financial Review*.

Katherine Brabon

I'm the author of the novels *The Memory Artist*, *The Shut Ins*, and the Stella prize shortlisted *Body Friend*. My work has received the Vogel's Literary Award, a NSW Premier's Literary

Award and the David Harold Tribe Fiction Prize. I live in Naarm/Melbourne.

Yenfay Camp

I am currently completing my Honours in English at the University of Sydney. Since early childhood, I have held a keen passion for not just reading books and poems, but writing them as well, an endeavour continuously supported with immense love by both my parents. My inspirations include Joan Didion, Sylvia Plath and Patti Smith. At eighteen, I became published with my debut collection of poems and short stories, *angel*. I hope to continue writing for the rest of my professional and private life.

Karen-Anne Coleman

I am a Research Affiliate and sessional academic working across multiple disciplines at the University of Sydney. My writing is concerned with how children and young people navigate a diverse world, and develop their own voices in it. This is an extension of my research and pedagogical interests, which include embodiment, gender, disability, diversity and inclusion. If you asked me what my relationship to writing is (as someone did in producing this abstract), I would say: complicated.

Joe Denman

I grew up in Lucknow, NSW, a small village outside of Orange in the Central West. I have always loved literature and reading, attending Kinross Wolaroi for my secondary education. I moved to the University of Sydney when I was eighteen to study a Bachelor of Arts and Advanced Studies (English/ Philosophy).

Eeshita

In a world that is always moving and changing, stories have helped me learn how to find my footing. Growing up in India, I have been surrounded by storytelling in its most vivid and diverse forms. I am also an alumna of the University of Sydney, which taught me how to weave all these tales into words on a page. And so, I believe my writing is a product of the places that have penned me in their unique inks. At the moment, I am pursuing MA in Publishing Media from Oxford Brookes University.

Tom Evans

I completed my Master of Publishing at the University of Sydney and now work in the book publishing industry. Inspired by books, I hope to inspire others with the joy of storytelling. I previously published several short stories in the last three anthologies.

Angela Fossi

I am a Sydney-based poet who lives with my partner and our cat. I hold a BA in English and Philosophy from the University of Sydney. I write poetry on themes of love, mental health, nature, spirituality, personal growth, and faith. Currently, I am studying for my MA in Creative Writing at the University of Sydney, where I hope to continue to develop my skills as a poet and a writer. This is my first publication.

Hellai Gul

I am a poet, critic, and writer. I am living and working on sovereign Burramattagal and Gadigal lands. My work can be found in *Sydney Review of Books*, *Cordite*, *Mascara*, *Foam:e*, and more. Connect with me via Insta: @hellai.gul.

Djuna Hallsworth

I am a Perth-born, Sydney-based writer and academic. I completed my PhD on the representation of motherhood in Danish film and television dramas, which is now published as a monograph entitled *Danish Mothers On-Screen*. I find that answering the question "What is your favourite movie?" with *Nymphomaniac* is a great way to start or end a conversation.

Dennis Haskell

I completed an Honours degree in English in 1976 and a PhD in 1981 at the University of Sydney. Since 1984 I have lived in Perth but I still remember my USyd experience with great affection. These poems reflect my memories of Sydney, where I grew up. My tenth poetry collection *Who Would Know?* was launched at the Perth Poetry Festival in August 2024. I am a Member of the Order of Australia for services to literature, especially poetry, and for intercultural understanding.

Ngoc Thuan Anh Huynh

I am a Sydney-based Vietnamese writer, poet, and student. Inspired by my identity journey and studies in psychology at the University of Sydney, my works have been centering queer romance, yearning, grief, and pondering on life in both Vietnamese and English. "Pines to write and yearns for fun" is my current motto. My articles and stories have been published on online self-publishing platforms and in *Honi Soit*, including "Obituary", which was shortlisted for the 2024 Writing Competition.

Sharmila Jayasinghe

I like to think of myself as a Sri Lankan-Australian writer or an Australian-Sri Lankan writer. That hyphenated label makes it that much easier for me to weave my stories incorporating mothers who fry fish cutlets in coconut oil, brides who wear seven necklaces on their wedding day, and children who eat avocado with sugar and milk powder, just as much about corporate sorts who wear stilettos and work in bustling cities and of those who turn new chapters in their lives without foresight into the cultural shock that awaits them.

Emoh Ebubechukwu Justina

I am a Nigerian writer who loves to express life experiences into metaphors of poetry and other forms of creative writing. This is my debut poetry piece in print.

Christina King

I am a writer from Sydney. I write historical fiction with a focus on the hidden lives of women in the eighteenth century. My short fiction and reviews have appeared in *Island* and *Lip* magazines. I won the Historical Novel Society of Australasia's 2019 short story contest with my colonial story "The Ink Stain". I am currently researching my PhD on the life of Dorothea Banks, the wife of botanist Joseph Banks. I am a passionate advocate for people living with Type 1 Diabetes.

Joshua Marcus

I am an avid reader and have had a keen interest in writing since I was a child, writing comic books and short stories. I took the time during the COVID-19 lockdown to write more, with the hope to one day publish a novel.

Alessio Maugeri

Ciao! Sono Alessio! I'm a twenty-year-old student here at USyd, studying Philosophy and Psychology. I've been writing as a hobby since I was fourteen, and since then it has been a fundamental part of my identity, my self-discovery, and my expression. My writing is deeply influenced by much of my life, whether that be the music I love, my culture and personal history, the ideas I ponder in class, the emotions that elevate or crush me, or the eternal, unyielding ache of lovesickness that my family plagues me with when they ask me if I've got a girlfriend yet. Basically, writing's my compass, my guide through all that is happy and haunting in the world, and in seeing it, I try to make it all beautiful. I hope that as you read my work, fiction or non-fiction, you can find something beautiful in it for yourself!

Matilda Meikle

I am a twenty-year-old author from Sydney. As a lesbian woman, I am passionate about sharing authentic queer narratives. My short stories have been recognised in a number of prizes including the Currency Press Award and the Nan Manefield Young Writer Award.

Toby A. Moffatt

I am a queer author from regional NSW. I am currently completing my final semester of a Master of Creative Writing at the University of Sydney. While primarily focused on writing poetry and prose regarding the imagined and real narratives associated with objects as well as the psychological trajectories surrounding significant affective events, "Attraction" is a first foray into the science fiction genre to explore isolation and belonging.

Holly May Myers

I am a second-year English and Marketing student at the University of Sydney, with a particular love for Oscar Wilde, Greta Gerwig films and rainy weather.

Sarah Nielsen

I am a writer and lawyer from Sydney and a graduate of the University of Sydney. I have recently completed a Graduate Certificate in Editing and Publishing at UTS. I had my publishing debut in the UTS Writers' Anthology and had the great joy of editing the UTS Writers' Anthology in 2024.

Nicholas Osiowy

I am an aspiring writer who relishes exploring particularity and perception. Born and raised in Sydney, I am inspired by urban and natural forms, and by writers from Matsuo Basho and Elizabeth Bishop to Gerald Murnane and Walt Whitman. I also enjoy swimming and unhinged dancing. My poetry and prose have appeared in *Booker*, *Diptych*, *1978*, *Pulp* and *Honi Soit*.

Siddhanth Pai

I am Siddhanth, an engineer who engineers poems from the worlds that lie within. I speak only one tongue, that of a poet. Broken and brave.

Chloe Isabelle Pryce

I studied a Bachelor of Arts (Languages) at the University of Sydney. After working first in the arts and entertainment industry, I returned to my alma mater, where I now write elaborate thank yous for a living. I enjoy writing melancholy little poems, swimming, and falling in love, and currently do all three on unceded Gadigal Country.

Saraa Purba

I am an Australian-Bengali aspiring writer from South Western Sydney. My work grapples with complications of familial dynamics and intergenerational trauma. Moreover, these experiences are captured through the lens of womanhood for me, as I probe at the visions of femininity asserted in Western and South Asian culture. Furthermore, I am on a quest to portray the nuances of love between such relationships, how our expectations of tenderness and aggression muddle in the face of reality.

Natarina Ramdhana

I am an Indonesian writer from Western Sydney who likes to experiment with different forms of writing. My work has been featured in publications such as *Playdough* and USyd's *Wattle Magazine*.

Sanskriti Satyakam

I am a doctoral candidate at the School of Communication in the Faculty of Arts and Social Sciences at the University of Technology Sydney (UTS). I study internet ontologies and cultures and especially like to explore self-curation and relational developments within social media communities. I sing for fun and post solo and collaborative pop covers on my Instagram @sanskritisatyakam. Although I seldom share my paintings online, I promise I am a decent painter.

Soralinn

I am currently a student at Usyd (Philosophy/International Business) originally from Burma. I began writing because I wanted to eternalise states of emotions, and find forgiveness in them.

Amalia Stone

I'm a Usyd alumni, BSc (Hons) 1996, LLB 1995, and a candidate for a Master of Creative Writing at UTS. I'm unpublished in relation to my creative work, extensively published in relation to intellectual property law, and write on Gadigal land.

Natalie Susak

I am a poet from Sydney, NSW. I have earned a Bachelor of Arts (Honours) in English and an MA Creative Writing from the University of Sydney. I edited poetry for *AVENUE* from

2022–23. I am interested in writing that explores postmemory and the beauties and horrors of nature. My work has appeared in *Cordite Poetry Review*, *Island*, *AVENUE*, and *Free the Verse*.

Simone Wong

I am a writer and poet studying English and Global Studies at the University of Sydney. I especially love to read and study international literature and hybrid forms.

Jannet Xie

I'm just a twenty-five-year-old Australian-born-Chinese trying to heal from new and old diagnoses; trying to figure out what things actually mean and navigating what my own growth should look like. I'm a past primary teacher, a future registered nurse, and will hopefully continue to do a lot of different things (too much at once, all at the same time).

Vanessa Yenson

I have been writing memoir essays since my brush with leukaemia twenty-seven years ago; however, I have recently found enjoyment in the freedom of writing fiction. I will sadly complete my Master of Arts in Creative Writing at the University of Technology Sydney (UTS) in 2024; however, I will continue learning and writing through the 2024 Novel Writing Course with Faber Academy. Along with scientific papers, I have published fiction in the *Lane Cove Literary*

Awards Anthology (2023), memoir pieces in the UTS Writers' Anthology *Soak* (2023), the SBS Emerging Writers' Competition Anthology *Emergence* (2023), the Hunter Writers' Centre's Grieve Anthologies (2015, 2017) and in the art and literature magazine *Art Ascent* (2019, 2021). In 2024, I had a fiction and memoir piece included in the UTS Writers' Anthology.

About the Editors

Urvi Agrawal

As an ode to all the times I have run into people or objects, nose buried in a book, and all the times I have found my oasis in language and words, I am here. A dreamer from Kathmandu, I am pursuing my Master of Creative Writing in this vibrant city. I am proud to be a part of this publication, my first anthology. My professional background includes consulting and marketing. Currently, I am interning at Sydney University Press.

Sophie Bellotti

I'm a reader, writer and editor living and working in Sydney across Wangal, Gadigal and Cammeraygal land. This is the third anthology I've had the pleasure of assisting with, and every year it is a joy and a privilege to work alongside the emerging writers whose words make up the project. Their stories and poetry demonstrate the power of language to foster community, connection and belonging.

Eeshita

Ever since I joined the anthology as a volunteer, I've been in awe of how much effort and devotion goes into publishing a piece of writing. With that sense of curiosity, I am now studying Publishing Media at Oxford Brookes University in the UK. It has been and will always be an honour being a part of the anthology's amazing editorial team and getting the opportunity to read some great stories from USyd's creative community.

Holly Ford

As a child I loved immersing myself in the fantastical worlds of books, from Hogwarts to Camp Half-Blood to Middle Earth. At that time I didn't realise how great an impact this passion would have on my life. Fast forward to now and I am working part-time as a Marketing Assistant at NewSouth Books while pursing a Master of Publishing at the University of Sydney. This is the second University of Sydney Anthology that I have worked on, and it has once again been a pleasure.

Komal Gupta

As a writer and proofreader for various writing groups I love helping authors perfect their writing to their desired outcome. As a writer myself I sympathise with the authors I help and I can understand how the author wants their work to sound. Through volunteering for the USyd Anthology I have had the privilege to support the visions of authors and the privilege to assist in the making of this book.

Hanna Holford

For as long as I can remember, I have loved reading and writing. Language has always fascinated me, especially since learning a second language – Swedish – at age nine. Growing up I was intrigued by how grammar and sentence structure worked, and I often scrutinised the books I was reading to figure out how the authors had constructed their prose. Unsurprisingly, I ended up studying publishing, in the hope of one day becoming an editor. I currently work at a second-hand bookstore in Paddington.

Shaan Lloyd

I am originally from South Africa and before pursuing a career in publishing, I was a secondary English teacher. I find joy in helping people and supporting writers to effectively communicate their ideas and experiences. I value lifelong learning and am passionate about empowering young people to develop a love for reading and creative writing. *Nothing Rhymes with Orange* is my first project with the University of Sydney Anthology.

Sumi Mahendran

After devouring books everywhere – dinner tables, long flights, train rides, and even those endless queues – I finally decided to switch from page-turning to word-polishing. Two decades of corporate life fund my survival, but my real love? Words! Whether it's reading in three languages or perfecting stories, literature has become my side hustle, and now I'm on a mission to turn rough drafts into polished gems.

Manuela Martin

Although I already have degrees in Media and Communication Management and International Management and Leadership, I decided to come back to what I have always loved and what was always there for me: books. This is also why I joined the University of Sydney Anthology team, where I am continuously learning and enjoying the work.

Nilab Siddiqi

As a life-long reader, it's no surprise that I've journeyed after a life in bookselling and publishing. I'm a proud Western Sydney creative who has spent the last few years nurturing my writing and artistic endeavours, and plan to continue to do so for as long as I can! My main creative and academic interests have been race, culture, and all the intersections in-between, and I'm currently focused on diversifying the writing and publishing industry in Australia!